ALPHA

A ROUGH SHIFTER ROMANCE

SARA FIELDS

COPYRIGHT

Copyright © 2020 by Stormy Night Publications and Sara Fields

All rights reserved. No part of this book may be reproduced or transmitted in any form or by any means, electronic or mechanical, including photocopying, recording, or by any information storage and retrieval system, without permission in writing from the publisher.

Published by Stormy Night Publications and Design, LLC.
www.StormyNightPublications.com

Fields, Sara
Alpha

Cover Design by Korey Mae Johnson
Images by Shutterstock/Serge Lee and Shutterstock/Krivosheev Vitaly

This book is intended for *adults only*. Spanking and other sexual activities represented in this book are fantasies only, intended for adults.

CHAPTER 1

awn

THE DAY I was taken changed my life forever.

They didn't even let me say goodbye.

When the government came for me, I was in the cell culture hood, splitting another flask of overly sensitive immune cells that I was planning to use in my next experiment. They stormed into the room in their black suits with their official-looking badges and guns on their hips, and they told me that I had to come with them right away. I didn't even have a chance to finish working with my cells.

They wouldn't identify what branch of the government they were associated with, but there was no question in my mind that they were quite high up. Maybe they were part of a CIA black site FBI team or the NSA or even some other group way up the ladder that normal people like me didn't even know about. One thing was for certain though, they meant business.

They'd cleared out my lab and sent my students, technicians, and post-docs home. It was empty as I was led out of my lab and back into the university halls with my very own security detail of at least a dozen different people. There wasn't another person in sight.

"What do you want with me?" I asked quietly. The government officials circled around me in a protective ring and not a single one of them answered as they corralled and forced me down the back stairwell in silence until we reached the ground floor. The University of Connecticut campus was uncharacteristically quiet on this Wednesday afternoon and I had a feeling it had everything to do with the men and women escorting me out of my lab and into a tinted black SUV. There were at least six other vehicles parked waiting for us and as I was coerced into one of them, the rest pulled up alongside us.

"Where are we going?" I asked again and one of the women stared back at me.

"You will be informed of your new position once we arrive at our final destination," she said, and I was at least grateful for a human voice.

"How long till we get there?" I questioned, knowing I was probably pressing my luck.

"A few hours. The jet is waiting on the tarmac as we speak," she answered evasively, and she didn't say anything more after that.

True to her word, she led me to a small airport that was under guard with soldiers in black-ops gear, all of them with rather heavy-looking assault rifles. There were several heavily armed soldiers surveying the area, but none of them seemed to be focused on threatening or intimidating me. Instead, everything and everyone seemed focused on protecting me.

Once we filed onto the runway, I got a look at the plane

waiting for us. It wasn't huge but its surface was covered in sheets of a strange-looking metal, likely to prevent anyone from being able to see it flying high in the sky. I assumed that it probably interfered with radar, making the aircraft virtually invisible to anyone looking for it.

High level government indeed.

I couldn't really get another look because I was led onto the plane at record speed.

In no time at all, the plane was up in the air. We were heading to wherever these people decided I needed to be.

I was led to a small table with leather bench seats on either side. There wasn't any other option but to take a seat, so I did. Then I waited for what would come next.

A tall woman with blonde hair slid into the seat across the table from me. Her austere demeanor spoke to her position and that she wasn't afraid of anyone or anything. Her hair was slicked back into a bun and not a single strand had fallen out of place on her head. Hazel eyes stared back at me, no nonsense and quite serious. Everything about her was somber and rigid and I knew at once that I was about to speak to one of the leaders of whatever organization had decided that I'd needed to be taken.

"Dr. Lowe, it is nice to finally meet you. My name is Amy Warren," the woman began.

"It's nice to meet you, Amy," I answered carefully.

"Now that we are in a contained airspace, it is safe to speak. What you are about to hear is intel of the highest classified level. It is dangerous information that could spark panic and paranoia throughout the United States, but not only that, it could terrify the rest of the world," she continued. My ears perked up and my brow furrowed with both confusion and concern.

I wasn't unused to the idea of keeping things secret. I'd worked in a number of institutions over the years and all of them had differing levels of secrecy. Competition amongst universities and private industries was vast, an underlying issue that I'd experienced in every single place I'd conducted my research. Working for the government would be something very different though. That much was quickly becoming obvious.

"What do you people want with me?" I replied. She ignored my aggressive tone.

"Dr. Lowe, you are one of the most respected stem cell biologists in the country. Not only that, but your work on both transformative mutations as well as your research into genetically modified organisms makes you an asset to the United States government. As such, your experience and especially your profile make you an ideal candidate to help us solve an issue that's been plaguing the country for several months now."

"This is a job interview then?"

"No. Not quite. Your cooperation is appreciated, but it is also compulsory. It is your duty as a scientist and as a United States citizen to do your due diligence and complete the task assigned to you," she replied curtly.

There was zero sarcasm or humor in her tone. She meant every single word and as I looked around at the serious faces around me, I knew that I was going to have little choice in what I had to do next.

"Am I going to be required to do anything illegal?" I questioned. "I won't take part in anything that might kill someone." My entire career had been focused on improving the human experience, using my research to help develop potential treatments for cancer, lupus, and especially in the handling of sickle cell disease, and I wasn't about to change that.

If they'd brought me in to work on weapons, they had another think coming. I wouldn't have any part of it.

"You won't be required to kill anyone," she replied. I noticed that she hadn't really fully answered my question.

"How did you come by my name and my work?" I asked next.

"Dr. Livingston recommended you."

I narrowed my eyes at her with suspicion.

Dr. Robert Livingston was my advisor from graduate school. I hadn't talked to him in a number of years, but I kept up with his publications here and there when I had a free afternoon. His work in stem cell research was world renowned and was one of the reasons I'd chosen him for my mentor in the first place. His findings laid the foundation of what I worked on today.

"Will I be working with Dr. Livingston?" I asked carefully.

"Yes. Your work with transformative mutations though will be especially useful to the research we are conducting and the answers we're looking for," she replied tersely.

"What exactly am I going to be working on?" I pressed. It was time to get down to business. It was clear that I didn't really have a choice from this point forward. Whatever it was, the work was important enough to be entirely classified and protected from public knowledge. In any case, it piqued my curiosity and I wanted to know more.

Amy took a deep breath and sighed.

"What I'm going to tell you next is a level of classified information that only a handful of people are aware of including the president and his closest advisors. Everyone else is kept almost entirely in the dark and only fed as much intel as they need to perform their jobs. Should you repeat this information, it will be considered treason under United States law and your immediate termination will follow," she warned.

She didn't elaborate on the definition of what termination might be, but there was little doubt in my mind that it meant that I would be assassinated if I opened my mouth.

My mouth went dry and I started to grow nervous.

"You've heard of the Department of Defense or the Department of Justice and the other various sectors of the United States government, but you haven't heard of the one I lead because on paper, it doesn't technically exist. The funding for my work has been stricken from all public record. There are very few people in the world that know of its existence at all," she continued.

I sat back and folded my hands into my lap.

"What is the name of your department?" I asked.

"I lead the Department of Paranormal Activity," she answered. Everything about her body language said that she was completely serious.

"Paranormal," I echoed. She had to be joking. Those things weren't real.

"Yes," she replied.

"As in ghosts and monsters and vampires and that sort of thing," I said, my disbelief more than obvious at this point.

"Our work very rarely deals with ghosts. Vampires hardly ever make waves as they are mainly solitary creatures unless they come together as a bonded pair. The list of monsters runs long though and would require much more of an explanation than you need," she explained.

"You're telling me these things actually exist, that they aren't just stories," I replied, my voice almost a whisper.

"I am," Amy nodded.

I tried to swallow my disbelief. I wouldn't have believed her if not for the technologically advanced plane we were currently traveling inside or the fully armed individuals sitting in the cabin with us and the fact that their organization had shut down the UConn campus, which was certainly a feat all by itself. As much as I wanted to disregard her explanation, I couldn't.

I should have been afraid at finding out this knowledge, but I wasn't. Instead, I was curious. All this time I'd thought these creatures were tales of folklore and myth, but as it turns out, parts of those stories may well be very true.

"It's your job to keep the public ignorant of the existence of these creatures and to handle them whenever they fall out of line," I said.

"It is," she replied.

"So, what do you need me for?"

"I assume you've heard of werewolves, yes?"

"I have."

"There are a group of creatures out there that are related to werewolves, we refer to them as Lycans, only they aren't constrained to changing under the moon. They're very strong and quite fierce, although not wholly invincible, and they've managed to kill a number of our soldiers. They shift into oversized wolves, probably at least double the size of a wild wolf. For several hundred years they've been a very docile group, but only very recently they've begun to act out. Once compliant and tame, they've become more aggressive and increasingly protective of their territories. They've begun to organize themselves into packs and that's only the ones we're aware of right now. My department has managed to capture a fair number of them, but several of them have managed to escape confinement. They're becoming a problem for us and we want to stop it before it gets out of hand. Your job is to find out why their behavior has suddenly changed," she explained.

"You want me to examine if there is a molecular reason for their changed behavior, if they're evolving," I replied carefully.

"Yes. We've collected a fair number of samples and have

quite a few more banked, but the experimental procedures are sensitive and Dr. Livingston has assured me that you would know how to proceed, that you have the very best hands for the job in the world," she responded.

I paused for a moment, processing everything she'd told me so far.

"You mentioned that you captured a few of these shifters?" I asked next.

"Yes. They refer to themselves as betas. According to our previous research, they are wolf-human hybrids, which is the reason we've been resistant to wiping them out before, especially since they haven't caused any large-scale problems for us. It's become difficult to handle those we have in captivity though and there is evidence that those in the wild are becoming much more brazen and aggressive as well. There's been quite a few that have broken out of our facilities. There's been deaths on the outside. We've had to explain a number of casualties as animal attacks, placing blame on mountain lions or coyotes or wolves instead."

"Where are you taking me?" I pressed. There was no more need for secrets from her.

"We're heading to a black site in the forests to the west of Helena in Montana. It's run by my department. Once we arrive, you'll be introduced to our labs and you'll be able to begin your research immediately. Dr. Livingston has been preparing for your arrival and has assured us that you can start right away," she replied.

I chewed my lip.

"You mentioned that the betas are not docile anymore. Is it safe to work with them or ask them questions?" I asked next.

"Yes. As long as you keep yourself out of their cages," she answered.

*　*　*

THE BLACK SITE location was well hidden within the mountains. Once the plane landed on the ground, I was funneled into yet another black tinted SUV that drove off into the countryside. At least ten others just like it surrounded us. After that, we drove off the road and into a tunnel that cut through a tall cliff side. The cars pushed onward through the northern Rockies and emerged onto a dirt road on the other side, well hidden from any eyes above that may be watching. The trees were thick as we wove in and around the mountains.

When we finally arrived at our destination, I barely had any time to appreciate how well concealed the facility was amongst the trees before I was led inside. What appeared to be a building only a couple of stories high descended well beneath the ground, hiding several floors of labs, offices, and meetings rooms underneath. It was really quite incredible.

Amy led me into an elevator at the back of the ground floor. We descended several levels to B6 where it stopped, we exited and climbed into a freight elevator that went even deeper. The screen indicating the floor went black and I no longer could tell where they were taking me. Amy scanned in with a keycard and the door finally opened, revealing the most magnificent lab I'd ever seen. I couldn't contain my surprise and my resulting gasp was quite audible between us. She led me out of the elevator after that, thankfully not commenting on the heated blush I could feel all over my face.

We walked into the most advanced scientific setup I'd ever encountered. The room was massive, practically the size of a warehouse, and segmented by bays of equipment. The closest bay was lined with a multitude of sequencers. The second had a number of flow cytometers and sorters and the third had mass spectrometers, as well as some machines that even I didn't recognize. There were a number of bays that I couldn't see down, but I had no doubt they were filled with the fanciest and newest tools that money could buy and probably a great deal more that weren't even available on the open market yet. There seemed to be billions of dollars' worth of scientific equipment hidden here deep underground in the northern reaches of the great Rocky Mountains.

It was a biologist's dream. Instead of waiting weeks to perform an experiment, I could do it myself in a matter of days. All in one centralized location.

I could get used to this.

Off in the distance, I saw a man working under a large clear plastic hood and I grinned, recognizing his thick white hair. It was Dr. Livingston. Amy led me over to him and he turned his head, smiled back, and put down his pipette. He had such a friendly face that always left me feeling comfortable, no matter if we were talking about life or arguing over differences in our hypotheses and that hadn't changed one bit in the time since I'd last seen him.

"Dr. Dawn Lowe, it's been a few years," he started, his eyes glowing with joy.

"It has been, hasn't it," I replied. I smiled in return and his grew even wider.

"I'd love to sit down for a coffee to catch up some time, but Amy here is a workhorse and she wants answers, so why don't you come with me," he said. "I'll take it from here," he told Amy and she nodded in agreement.

"Anything you two need, you just let me know," she replied. "It was nice to meet you, Dr. Lowe. I'll look forward to working with you." With that, she handed me a keycard. It had both my name and face on it. Apparently, they'd been prepared for my arrival long before today. I clipped it onto my lab coat and thanked her politely, even if nothing about this had been my choice.

She didn't say anything more, turning on her heels and returning to the freight elevator. Once it closed, I sighed.

"Well, it's been a day," I started, swinging my gaze to meet Livingston's soft brown ones.

"I bet it has. Why don't you and I go into the specimen hold and I can introduce you to the creatures we're studying. I imagine you have your doubts about the truth of what Amy has told you so far, so let's get that out of the way first," he suggested.

Of course, he was right. Even though I'd seen all this circumstantial evidence to suggest that paranormal life existed and was worth protecting in secret, it still didn't feel quite real or tangible in any way. It felt like a story and the fastest way to make it a reality would be to see it myself.

"How did they find you?" I asked as he led me down the bay of sequencers to the back, where there was a large metal door. He swiped his own keycard and it slid open. The two of us walked inside. We were greeted with another pair of doors. After walking through those, we were met with a third set before we walked down a long hallway. Finally, we passed through a fourth set of doors before the hallway opened up into a much larger room, only instead of scientific equipment, this was lined with large glass cells.

I froze. Inside each one of them was a person.

"These are the shifters you're going to be studying, Dr. Lowe," Livingston said.

"Call me Dawn," I answered.

I looked around and they didn't appear as dangerous as Amy had led me to believe. In fact, many of them looked far too human.

"Come, let me introduce you to Rebecca. She's the most docile of the bunch and the only one that I'm comfortable with going into her cell. As long as she isn't threatened, her ability to keep her instincts at bay is second to none amongst her kind," he added.

I followed him down the row of individual enclosures. They were all standalone glass cages, situated next to each other with at least three feet in between each one. It was clear that the glass was reinforced, perhaps bulletproof or strong enough to contain a bomb, but I wasn't certain. As we walked through the cells, I assessed the creatures kept inside and I began to notice a few things that definitely weren't human. The males were quite a bit larger than normal human men would be. The females were slender and sized similarly to human women, but they appeared strong in their own right. All of their irises were flecked with yellow, perhaps an indication of their human-wolf hybrid status. Some of them met my eyes with open hostility, others with indifference, and only a few looked back at me with curiosity.

The whole thing was quite disconcerting.

The very last cell in the block held a petite woman. Her eyes were brown and unlike the others, only slightly flecked with yellow. Long chocolate brown hair hung in waves down to her waist. She looked at me suspiciously, studying my face as I did hers. Livingston scanned his card outside her cell and the glass door slid open. We walked inside and the door slid closed behind the two of us.

I couldn't help feeling slightly uneasy at being trapped inside a cell with a beast.

"Rebecca, it's good to see you again," he offered, and she smiled, if a bit coldly. She turned her head toward me, and her eyes narrowed slightly as she evaluated my presence more closely. Then she sniffed the air and her eyes opened a bit wider. Her expression grew inquisitive after that. I couldn't sense any hostility.

"Dr. Livingston," she greeted, all while keeping her eyes locked on me.

"This is Dr. Dawn Lowe. She's come to work with me. If you're willing, I'd love for you to show her what you're capable of," he said gently. He didn't demand anything or make a move in her direction. Instead, he just simply made a suggestion to her as if he was talking to a friend instead of a prisoner deep in a secret government prison.

"I would, but I want to do it with her here with me. Alone," Rebecca replied, staring right into my eyes. She didn't shift her gaze to Livingston, not even for a second. Instead, she remained focused entirely on me. I had to repress the shiver of nervous fear that threatened to race down my spine.

"Why is that?" he pressed cautiously.

"Because I think Dawn and I are going to be great friends," she answered evasively. To her credit, I sensed no aggression. If anything, she was curious or maybe even cautiously friendly. Nothing in her demeanor suggested that she wanted to attack me, but I did feel like she wanted to tell me something and that she didn't want Livingston to hear what she had to say. I wanted to know what that was.

I just hoped that in this instance, curiosity didn't kill the cat.

"Dawn?" he asked me, and I turned to look back at him.

"It's fine. Why don't you return to your experiments? I'll talk with Rebecca for a little while and then I'll come find you so that we can finish our little chat."

There was an armed guard walking by at that moment with a massive gun that looked a lot like a flamethrower, so even if it did prove dangerous, I had faith that he'd rescue me before Rebecca ripped out my throat. At least, I hoped he would.

"Are you sure? The shift can be quite shocking when you

see it for the first time," he said carefully. His face tightened with concern.

"Don't worry, I'll be fine," I smiled. He sighed, nodded, and scanned his card again before exiting the enclosure. Rebecca and I watched as he left the room, the surrounding silence oppressive in its intensity.

When he was out of sight, I sighed and sat down in a wooden chair that was by the card table in the corner. Rebecca sat across from me, the movements of her body graceful and still cautious.

"Now that he's gone, he won't be able to hear what we say," she said softly, sitting back in her chair. She cocked her head to the side, sniffing the air once more.

"Why do you want to talk to me alone?" I asked as nonthreateningly as I could.

"Your scent is very unique. I've only smelled something like it once before and it's further confirmation of what I already knew was happening," she answered.

"What is happening?"

"The alpha has finally returned for us and he's going to be coming for the betas and his mate. Once he scents his omega, he's going to take her as his," she responded.

"And who is this omega?"

"Oh, Dawn, that omega is you."

CHAPTER 2

awn

I WAS TAKEN ABACK for a long second.

"What are you talking about?" I asked. When she didn't answer right away, I continued and tried to explain myself, sure that what she was saying didn't make any sense.

"I'm just a biologist who the government decided was useful to the research they're conducting here. I've only just arrived. I haven't even been here an hour yet. My job is to simply figure out why the shifters' behavior has changed," I probed. Her lip curled up in a suggestive smirk.

"The betas are restless. I'm restless too. I'm a lower beta with less of a genomic percentage of wolf than the others, so I haven't felt it as strongly as they have, but it's still there. I can feel the presence of an alpha out there and now that I know you exist, that just confirms it twofold," she replied rather assuredly.

"How can you be so sure?"

"All of the betas are connected. There's an energy we feed off of in the trees, in the water, in the very air we breathe. It binds us together as one and when our alpha rises, we answer. He calls for us and he calls for his mate. We hear that call no matter what."

I felt uneasy. I didn't know what to think of this information. Thrust into a world that I didn't understand, I sat back and just stared at her.

"I want to see what makes you a shifter. Will you show me?" I finally asked.

"Of course. Just," she hesitated, "don't scream." After that, she started to strip, and I kept silent.

Quickly and efficiently, she pulled the gray t-shirt over her head and then pushed her leggings down her waist. Reaching behind her back, she unclasped her bra and then slipped her panties over her hips. She undressed completely in front of me and I averted my eyes in order to preserve her modesty.

"Don't look away," she demanded.

"It doesn't bother you?"

"No. It's normal when you are part of the pack," she replied. "If we don't get naked before we shift, our clothes end up in tatters and then we just have to get new ones all the time. Here, sometimes that takes days so we're all rather comfortable with our nakedness, but there's no reason to destroy our clothes when it's not really necessary."

This was certainly new to me though. I hadn't really been around any woman this naked since the girl's locker rooms back in high school. It felt incredibly odd to be thrust into a situation like this.

Her slender form was taut with finely toned muscles. Pert breasts gave way to a firm stomach and shapely hips. She had a physique that most women would kill to have.

"I'm going to shift now," she said softly. "Don't be afraid."

ALPHA

I tried to prepare myself.

Her nails were the first thing to change, lengthening at a frightening speed into thick sharp claws. Then her back began to round and I heard the sickening sound of her vertebrae popping and cracking, changing shape and forcing her arms toward the floor. Next, her ribs fractured and rounded into more of a barrel shape and her head flew back as a scream gradually transformed into a howl. Dark brown hair sprouted all over her skin and I quickly realized that it was very thick fur. Her fingers snapped and shortened, and her hands morphed into paws that clawed at the floor beneath them.

The most haunting thing about it aside from the sound of breaking bones was when her nose started to lengthen into a snout. Her eyes changed from golden flecked brown to fully yellow as a tail sprouted from the base of her spine.

The whole change occurred in less than ten seconds. Just moments before, a naked human woman had stood before me and now a massive beast had taken her place.

Amy had been right. Rebecca's wolf form was at least double if not triple the size of a normal wolf and if she followed the general rules of nature, she was undoubtedly smaller than the male counterpart of her species. I stood up slowly and took a tentative step toward her before pausing. She stood at eye level with my chest. I wasn't sure if she'd attack me in this form. One strategic bite could kill me in seconds.

I didn't feel quite so confident anymore in the guard outside the cage as I stared into the yellow eyes of such a massive animal.

She nodded though and I was reminded of her human origins.

I took another step and reached for her, tracing my fingers along her snout and then in between her eyes. After that, I walked down the length of her body, running my palm down the base of her spine and then down her tail.

"You are incredible," I observed, and she snorted in what I imagined was a sound of amusement. Her fur was coarse and thick, yet astonishingly smooth and elegant. The brown of her fur matched the brown of her hair, but it was also pigmented with patches of blacks and gray. It was a beautiful coat.

She turned and stared into my eyes.

"Do you hear me, omega?"

Unexpectedly, Rebecca's voice rang out in my head, but her lips didn't move. She didn't howl or even make a noise, but I still heard her all the same. It was more than a little unnerving.

"I can," I answered, and her cheeks rose up in what I could only imagine a wolf smiling would look like. Her eyes warmed toward me and the coldness I had initially felt from her fell away completely.

"So, it's true then, you are the omega. If you weren't, there would be no way I could communicate with you in this form." She sat back on her haunches and her tail wagged back and forth slowly. For a moment, she reminded me of something distinctly feline even though she was very different from a cat.

"What does being an omega even mean?"

"The omega," she corrected. *"It means that the alpha has risen. Every few hundred years, the alpha rises to lead us and to spread the seed of our kind. Without our alpha, our species would die out. There hasn't been an alpha in existence since the early 1600s."*

"Why is that?"

"Betas are infertile, at least they are after several generations or they reach a certain age. Every wolf in this room with me is incapable of siring children."

"What does that have to do with me?"

"You are special. Through mechanisms we do not understand, when an alpha rises, so does an omega, or in other words, his fated mate. Something in your DNA responds to him, maybe something epigenetically repressed that is activated once you're in his presence or maybe it is through some other mechanism, but it really doesn't matter. Your existence is direct evidence that our alpha has risen. I had felt him in my bones, but I was reluctant to believe it was real."

"How do you know all this?"

"Because I was living in Rome when the last alpha rose."

I stilled. That would mean she was more than three hundred years old.

"I was born in the year 1645. I stopped being fertile in 1701."

Holy shit. This was a scientific anomaly like nothing I had ever seen.

"The alpha is going to be coming for us and for you, once he realizes you're here. He won't tolerate the captivity of his betas and he will free us. It won't be long. I can feel he isn't far and that he will bring the power of the pack with him. He won't come alone. They'll destroy this facility in an effort to give the betas the freedom to follow their alpha, just like nature intended."

"How have you survived this long?"

"We're strong and we're intelligent. The humans think they have us secure down here, but it is our nature to evaluate everything for a weakness. We have been biding our time until the alpha rises and that time is now. We only have to wait for him to arrive to help us take back our freedom."

"How do you know the alpha is coming for you? And for me?"

"I can feel him coming for us. I can also feel his anger but most of all, I can feel his hunger to find his mate. You'd best prepare yourself, omega, because when he comes for you, he's never going to let you go."

* * *

When I returned to Livingston, I didn't tell him what Rebecca had told me, just that she had explained what her kind were and that she had wanted to get to know me on a woman to woman level. He'd taken my word at face value and then, in his excitement to have me here, proceeded to show me the rest of the lab and the resources I had at my disposal. I found myself only partially listening, my mind too wrapped up in what Rebecca and I had discussed. Finally, when he sensed my detachment, he looked at his watch. It was nearly eight o'clock and I hadn't eaten a thing since breakfast. My stomach chose that moment to voice its displeasure and growled loudly in protest. Livingston chuckled and his eyes sparkled with amusement at hearing it.

"Look at the time! I'm sure you're exhausted and pretty hungry. I'll show you to your room, and let me tell you, this place has the most fantastic room service. Pretty much whatever you want, whenever you want. It's so incredibly good!" he exclaimed. "It's not far, follow me."

True to his word, he brought me to a small apartment that was only a few minutes' walk away from the lab. There, he showed me the room service menu and pointed out his favorites, which happened to be the berry-glazed French toast and the chefs specially made cinnamon pancakes. I grinned, remembering just how much of a sweet tooth my former mentor had. Apparently, some things never change.

"It's good to see you again, Dawn. I'm looking forward to working with you, just like old times," he exclaimed elatedly.

"As am I," I answered, smiling in return.

He didn't stay much longer, only to point out essential information like what floors I didn't have access to and the fact that the lab was shut down after midnight unless explicit permission was obtained first.

After Livingston retired to his own quarters, I picked up the phone and ordered the French toast he'd liked so much, only I added eggs and sausage to my order. I didn't care that it was dinnertime. I was going to have breakfast because I wanted to.

It had been a day and sometimes sugar made it all better. The only thing better would have been sex, but I hadn't had that in years thanks to my work.

I didn't know what I was going to do with the information I had learned just yet, but I would deal with it in the morning. Funny little thing about science, sometimes even the very best things in life got put on the backburner because the next grant was due, the next manuscript needed to be submitted, and more data was required for either one or even both at the exact same time. Science never slept, but I certainly was going to tonight.

* * *

I woke up early that morning exhausted. Blinking my weariness away, I stared at the digital clock on the nightstand. It read 5:00 a.m. It wasn't time to get up yet. No way.

I closed my eyes and groaned as I wondered what had woken me up in the first place. I curled up into the soft mattress, pulling the covers up and over my shoulders as a shiver raced down my spine. Just as I began to drift back into dreamland, the bed shook beneath me, and my eyes shot open.

What the hell was that?

It happened again and I started to grow uneasy. Here I was, several floors underground, and the ground was quaking above and below my feet. Was this building reinforced against an earthquake? Did Montana even get those? Was the ceiling going to fall down and bury me alive?

I groaned. I wanted to go back to sleep, but my mind was racing too fast to even contemplate it.

I didn't want to die for the sake of whatever research I'd been forced into. Feeling suddenly way more awake than I did before, I hopped out of bed and hurried to turn on the light. I rushed to get dressed, finding a pair of jeans, a tank top, and a long-sleeved button-up flannel shirt in forest green. Everything was a perfect fit. The government had my sizes apparently and had filled up a closet with clothes for me to my exact specifications. I didn't know whether to be creeped out or impressed.

The entire building rattled again, and a hairline fracture raced across the ceiling above me. I gritted my teeth and stared up at it.

Oh, fuck this! I wasn't going to be buried alive in a secret government coffin. I needed to get above ground right now.

I pulled on a pair of socks and a pair of hiking boots and quickly packed a backpack of essentials, like a few water bottles, snack bars, and some spare clothes that I found in the room. In no time at all, I was running out that door and back into the freight elevator that had taken me down here in the first place. Once I got to the highest floor that the elevator went, I burst out of it and straight into what I could only describe as hell on Earth.

The sound of gunfire popping indoors was deafening and I instinctually ducked for cover, unsure exactly where it was coming from. Men in black-ops combat gear ran forward in units of two and three and even larger groups, sprinting out from more elevators and what I could only imagine were stairwells, but that wasn't even remotely the worst of it.

At least thirty massive wolves were sprinting across the enormous room. These wolves were larger than Rebecca had been, some standing at more than five feet tall. If one of them stood eye to eye with me, I'd be able to stare right back at them without having to look up or down. They were that big.

The combat officers aimed their weapons at the wolves and pulled the triggers, but the bullets just bounced off their flesh. Not a single one passed through the beasts' thick fur, allowing them to carry on in their attack without even a scratch. It was terrifying and mesmerizing all the same. The more I watched them move and fight, the more I realized that humans were certainly no longer at the top of the food chain.

These wolf shifters were. Together, as a pack, they were formidable, maybe even invincible. I was witnessing the beginnings of a battle and I very much thought the humans were not going to win this day.

At first, the gunfire scared me. Then I saw a giant black wolf tear the head right off of a man with his teeth. The crunching sound of his spine breaking and ripping apart was sickeningly loud and wet. Blood sprayed across the floor, staining the pristine white tile with red.

That's when I recognized that the floor was already slick with it. A number of bodies lay motionless on the floor, in pools of blood that were growing larger and larger by the second. For several moments, I just stared at the blood until I forced myself to look away from both the bodies and the carnage.

The wolves had come here, and I was the only human who knew why. The alpha had risen and had come for his betas, but that's not the only thing he was coming for. I had to move. Rebecca had said that the alpha would come looking for me and I didn't want to be found. So far, no one had noticed my presence because they were too caught up in battle to be paying attention to a lone woman slinking along the wall and I was extraordinarily grateful for that.

The stench of blood was metallic and strong,

compounded with the smell of death. I doubted the wolves could sense me because of it. The operatives didn't care because I was human too and I didn't pose a threat to them.

Cautiously, I moved around the corner of a hallway and stepped carefully so that my boots were silent against the white tiles. I stuck close to the wall and kept out of sight. Once I was sure I was safe from prying eyes, I dashed down the hallway to find an open security office door and looked inside. There was no one there but I saw something that could prove useful in my journey back to the upper levels.

There was a Taser on the table. I had nothing to protect myself, so I took it.

There were a couple of computers that were powered on and I gazed over to them, seeing the active security footage of the compound. Every screen was lit up with humans and wolves engaging in battle. One of them was the holding room where Rebecca and the other betas were held. I narrowed my eyes and watched them pace back and forth in their cells, almost like they were waiting for a sign, and then all at once, they changed into their wolf forms. I watched as each one of them shifted in their cells and burst forward, all striking their cages at the exact same spot at the lower right of the entryway door. At first, it didn't appear as though anything had happened at all, but after a few long seconds, the very first crack splintered across the glass. And then another.

Every single wolf dove at their door once again and the glass holding them captive shattered into pieces. It was a coordinated attack that destroyed the entrance to each cage, allowing the wolves to walk out unhindered. There wasn't even a single guard in the room because they were all here on this floor fighting off the wolf attack from above.

The alpha had come, and he'd brought a war with him.

Amy was going to have a field day covering up this one,

but I wasn't going to stick around long enough to find out exactly how it ended. I stuffed the Taser in my back pocket and went back out into the hallway, following it down to the very end where I found an empty stairwell. It was locked, but when I swept my badge in front of the electric panel on the right side of it, I heard the locks disengage beneath its metal surface. When I grasped the doorknob this time, it opened with ease. I burst up the stairs two at a time, not keeping track of how many floors I climbed. Soon enough, I reached the top and emerged out of an even thicker metal door straight into the forest. There was no one out here, which told me that I must have found a back door of some kind. Up here, it was silent. There were no indications of the war happening down below. Just the songs of birds, the buzzing of bugs, and the rustling of the leaves in the breeze. It was peaceful.

I didn't have a plan now that I was up here, so I'd have to come up with one. I looked around and noticed that there was a well-worn dirt trail that led away from the door, so I stepped down the few stairs and followed it into the trees. The best thing for me to do now was to hide out until the wolves left and then I could return to the black site and see who was left.

I hope Livingston hadn't been hurt. I also hoped that Rebecca had gotten out.

That wasn't all I hoped for though.

I hoped that the alpha would come and go without me.

I walked down the path, making as little noise as possible by avoiding any twigs, branches, or dried leaves on the ground. The scene I had just left had been quite horrifying, but up here, it felt like just a fading nightmare. The sky was just beginning to brighten from the rising sun, soft oranges and brilliant reds chasing away the dark of night. As the day lightened, the birds began to sing louder and the bugs quieted. I'd always loved walking through the woods and this time it felt even more serene because of the carnage I'd just run away from.

I'd find a place to hide and I'd come out when the wolves were gone. The alpha wasn't going to find me out here.

CHAPTER 3

iba

When I had awakened for the first time, I could sense her. She'd been put on this earth for me and me alone and nothing was going to stop me from getting to her. Her scent and the connection to my pack were the only things I'd ever known. For me, it was instinct and there was nothing more powerful than that.

I was *the* alpha.

I wasn't like other humans. I hadn't been born to a woman nor was I the product of a she-wolf's birth. No. I was different.

I was formed from the very essence of the earth itself, a magical combination of virility and power personified into a predator that was unmatched in this world. I was the first full-blooded alpha in centuries, and I was ready to take control of my mate and my pack. It was my responsibility to ensure the continuation of our species and I had every intention of doing exactly that, no matter what got put in my way.

I could feel the magic of nature running through my veins. The lifeblood that pumped through my heart was powered by the energy created by the rushing water that cut through rock, the liquid magma that carved the surface of the planet, and the wind that rustled through the leaves of the trees.

I was wolf. I was life itself. I was alpha.

When I had walked out of the cave that had given me life, my betas had already been on their way. They'd detected my existence and come to me when I had called for them. Now there were fifty in my pack and more were arriving every day.

But there were more that couldn't come because they were behind bars. More of my people were trapped in captivity and I had to get them out. I wouldn't stand for the unfair imprisonment of my kind, not when I could do something about it.

The connection between me and my betas was strong and unbreakable. I gave them direct orders and they obeyed or else the alpha bond reminded them who was in charge. They answered to me and me alone. Nature demanded it.

My omega was another story. She was my mate and she was human, but she would learn that she would answer to me too.

I'd risen deep in the mountains not long ago and stayed sedentary as my pack had come to me. The past several days I'd sensed a segment of my pack not far off and I had been making plans to rescue them. Yesterday though, I'd scented her on the wind.

My mate.

And I had come for her.

She wasn't far. I could feel her steps on the earth, could scent her breath on the air. I knew she was close, and I was going to find her. And then I was going to teach her of her rightful place.

My pack and I had acted early in the morning, catching the humans unawares for the most part. It had been surprisingly easy to break into the compound. One of my wolves had knocked out a security guard and stolen his badge. Once we had snuck into the facility, we had stolen several more keycards and gained access to the entire building, which we found went deep underground.

Through my connection to my trapped betas, I'd sent them a message that we were coming for them. They'd begun their own escape from several floors below on my command. The building's alarm had been triggered in the process and that's when the humans had started their attack. We shifted into our wolf forms immediately. We'd been able to detect them coming and we'd been ready. Their strategies were simplistic and uncoordinated, and it had been easy for us to break through their ranks.

They'd used guns, which had proven useless against us when in wolf form. Our hides were thick and impenetrable, except to one very particular material.

Silver. A blade or a bullet made from the precious metal would pierce right into our flesh. This place hadn't stocked up on such resources, that much was becoming increasingly obvious. We were more vulnerable when in our human forms, our skin being much more exposed and defenseless against weapons. Once any danger presented itself, we would shift and were much safer because of it.

I'd instructed my people not to kill needlessly, but the numbers of humans proved to be large and even though we were protected from normal bullets, we were not immune to fire. They used a fair number of grenades and flamethrowers and several of my people were hurt. The betas defended themselves and once the captives from down below joined our ranks, we'd pulled out. I didn't want to be there any longer than necessary.

I'd given the command to escape this place and make camp several miles away where they'd be safe. I'd instructed them to leave without me because I had my own mission to complete. I'd come back on my own. I'd come to find my mate.

I sniffed the air and her scent carried on the breeze. It was sweet, an aroma of apples and peaches and fragrant wildflowers and as refreshing as rain. I took a deep breath and savored the moment, knowing she was close.

It was my destiny to find her. Fate demanded it. Now it was only a matter of time.

A twig cracked in the distance. The birds went silent. The fur on my back raised in excitement. I began to run. She was out there, and she wasn't far. I could feel it.

I sprinted through the forest, my paws falling silently onto the dirt beneath me. I wove through the trees in stealth, ensuring that every step was as noiseless as possible. I was the predator and she was my prey. She wasn't going to know that I had found her until I wanted it to be known. Until then, I was going to enjoy the chase.

As I came across her traveled path, it quickly became clear that she hadn't been trained in the ways of the forest. She did nothing to conceal her footsteps or the branches and leaves that had been broken or pushed aside as she made her way through the brush. It was easy to track her this way, and I loped along her trail until I knew she was very near.

I slowed down, padding softly down the defined dirt path until I saw the blue of her jeans and the green of her shirt peeking through the brush. Carefully, I circled around so that I could see her face for the very first time.

I sat on my haunches and licked my lips. I waited as she came around the bend, striding slowly through the forest as though she didn't have a care in the world, like she didn't know I was coming for her. Maybe she did or maybe she didn't. Maybe she just thought she was safe.

She wasn't. Not from me. She'd never be safe from me again.

She lifted her eyes finally and came to an abrupt stop, pulling in a panicked gasp as she took in the sight of me. Her fingers clutched at her chest and she whined so softly that it was almost imperceptible, but I heard it anyway.

I'd found her and now she was mine.

My mate.

Perfection.

Deep green irises regarded me with surprise, flecked with gold and hazel around her dark human pupils. A small nose and a pointed chin gave her an air of delicacy. Her cheekbones were flushed from the effort of her hike and it only served to deepen her beauty. Soft, elegant mahogany waves hung to her waist and I yearned to trace my fingers through every strand. I longed to pull it hard, force her lips to mine, and kiss her like she was meant to be kissed. I wanted to do a great many more things, but none of them involved her fully clothed. I licked my lips, imagining her beautiful little body naked. She wasn't very tall, but her body was well formed. Her breasts would fit in the palm of my hand and I wondered if her nipples would be a pretty pink or a lovely tan color. It wouldn't be long until I found out. Her slender waist gave way to curvy hips and I salivated at the thought of the taste of her on my tongue.

There was something deep in her eyes that I hadn't expected though.

Defiance.

She didn't know her rightful place. She would soon though. She was my omega and I was her alpha and nothing was ever going to change that.

It was time I taught her exactly that.

CHAPTER 4

*D*awn

THE WOLF STANDING AHEAD of me on the path was the most majestic creature I had ever seen. For a moment, I just stood there dumbfounded, taking in the sight of him. A streak of terror raced through me and I immediately pushed it away, unwilling to showcase my fear in front of such a dangerous and unpredictable beast. He was the supreme predator and he'd be able to sense my terror from a mile away. I had no doubt he would take advantage of that if he noticed even the slightest hesitation.

I couldn't stop myself from admiring such an elegantly powerful animal though.

The first thing I noticed was his irises, which were unlike the yellow-eyed betas I'd encountered earlier. They were a brilliant ice blue that reminded me of some of the bluest waters of the ocean, multifaceted and glittering like freshly cut gemstones. His coat was deep shadow and flecked with gray and white, which made him seem all the more magnificent while also extremely dangerous. He was much larger than the others, so when he was sitting at full height, he was much taller and certainly much stronger than me. If I stood right next to him, the top of my head would only reach the bottom of his chin. He carried with him an air of expectancy as he watched me, and his demeanor gave the distinct impression that he was used to being obeyed. Even more so, he expected me to obey him.

I knew who he was. This was the alpha and he'd found me.

I'd been naïve thinking that I could escape and that he wouldn't be able to track me down. I'd seen the battle below. I'd witnessed how the wolves had taken the advantage and I'd known the humans were fighting hard, but they were going to lose. I should have known that I would too.

He growled softly, the sound somewhat tender and also terrifyingly haunting in the same breath. It rumbled deep down into the pit of my soul and I felt myself begin to answer. My heart started to pound, and my blood raced. Shamefully, my nipples peaked inside my bra and the seat of my panties dampened with arousal.

This couldn't be happening. I wouldn't let it.

He transformed right before my eyes, changing into his human form in a fraction of a second. If I had been looking away, I would have missed the whole thing.

His eyes remained just as hauntingly blue. I tried to ignore the fact that he was completely naked, but it was so very difficult.

"Omega," he breathed, his voice low and chilling and deeply arousing.

He wasn't any less majestic in human form than he was in wolf form. A perfect specimen of a man, he stood over six feet tall with exceptionally well-defined muscles. His biceps were thick, and I absentmindedly wondered if I could fit my hands around them. Corded muscles flexed as he assessed me, likely deciding whether to pounce with aggression or to approach me with caution. A thick beard covered his chin, but it only highlighted the strong, firm cheekbones just above it. Thick brows made his eyes seem dark and ominous as they stared back at me, which only made my body react even more strongly to his cool appraisal.

Muscled thighs rippled with tension as he debated his next move. But everything paled in comparison to his cock.

It was enormous and very, very hard. My pussy clenched as I imagined taking a man of his girth inside me and even though I feared how much it might hurt, I was terrified of just how much I would enjoy it. Of how much I might actually want it.

I wasn't that girl. I couldn't be.

I'd always worked hard. All my life, I'd been exclusively career minded and focused on nothing else. I'd been the good girl. When there was homework assigned, I'd always been the one to turn it in early. When there was a group project, I took the lead and helped everyone organize. I'd never gone out on the weekends and partied, nor had I ever let myself stray off the path to success. I had always met my deadlines, no matter if it had meant an all-nighter or the entire weekend spent in the library.

I'd never let myself get distracted by sex.

This man was different. He seemed like he knew how to make a woman fall to her knees and that scared me, but I was also horrified that it made me wet.

There was a certain primal intensity in the way he stared at me, almost like he would devour me whole in a fraction of a second, as if he could undo me with a simple twitch of his fingers. Underneath all that though was a certain tenderness as he looked at me. I imagined those big arms enveloping me as he raised my chin and kissed me like I wanted to be kissed. I licked my lips, finding myself unsure of him.

I shifted back and forth from foot to foot, uncertain of my next move. He didn't appear to be in any rush to be the first to react either, so the two of us appeared to be in some sort of standoff. I sniffed the air and my tongue watered as his scent carried on the breeze.

It was masculine and strong, complete and utter perfection.

Unexpectedly, my core clenched hard, twisting in on itself with pain and unwelcome pleasure. My pussy tightened and I cried out silently in alarm. What the hell was happening to me? I'd never been this aroused in my life simply at the sight of a naked man. I wasn't sure what to do.

"Do you feel it, little omega? Do you feel your body answering to your alpha's call?" he murmured, and I could feel my shoulders rounding forward, almost like my body wanted to submit to him. I froze once I realized what I was doing, horrified at myself.

I wanted to run. I needed to get out of here.

I couldn't do this. I wouldn't. He wasn't going to take me as his. I belonged to no one, least of all him.

I remembered the Taser in my back pocket. I had something to fight with just in case things went badly for me. He would pay if he tried to touch me. I would make sure of it.

I took one step back and then another.

"Don't you run, little omega. You won't like what happens if you do," he warned gently.

I highly doubted I would like it if he caught me at all. As soon as he got close to me, he'd probably take exactly what he wanted and by just how hard his cock was, I could guess that it didn't involve just a simple handshake. He probably wanted much more than I was willing to give. I had little doubt that he wanted to fuck me.

I wasn't going to let him catch me.

Without hesitation, I started running backwards, pivoted and darted away as quickly as I could. I put everything I had into running down that path, ensuring that I didn't catch my foot on a wayward root or a loose rock. I bolted like my life depended on it because right now, it very much did.

I heard him running behind me, his footfalls soft in the brush unlike mine. I didn't try to hide my escape because it was no longer necessary. I just ran. I didn't look back either.

"Keep running, little omega. I'm going to enjoy teaching you a lesson about hierarchy once I inevitably catch you."

His voice rang out in my head like a siren and my body reacted on an almost visceral level to its call. My pussy clenched down hard and my nipples pebbled with desire. For a moment, I contemplated letting him catch me just to see what might happen, but I pushed that thought aside almost as quickly as it appeared.

It was just arousal. I had to stop thinking with my pussy. I had to think with my mind.

I snarled loudly, voicing my displeasure at his presence in my head.

"I see you're a feisty one then. I'm going to enjoy making you break for me. I'm especially going to enjoy the look on your face when I make you scream my name as you come for me too."

Fucking cocky bastard.

I ran harder, giving it all I had. I looked back and I saw him chasing me. He was in his wolf form and my face fell. He was gaining on me far more quickly than I anticipated. I had to do something. Fast. I approached a clearing and when I reached the opposite side, I used a tree trunk to swing around, grabbed the Taser out of my pocket, and rounded back on him. I was ready to fight. If I was going to be taken, I wasn't going to make it easy on him. Not even in the slightest.

He stalked closer to me, taking one step at a time until he was a scarcely a few feet away from me. I gritted my teeth as he shifted back into his human form so close to me that I could feel the prickle of magic on my skin. I swallowed heavily and lifted my arms, preparing myself to fire the Taser, all the while trying not to rub my fingers on my tingling flesh.

It was similar to a gun in shape and form. I curled my fingers around the grip, pressing a single finger against the trigger. I cupped my other hand beneath it, holding it in place just in case there was any kickback. It was simple enough to figure out, but I'd never fired one before, so I believed it was better to be safe than sorry.

"Don't come any closer," I warned.

"Or else what, my little mate?" he dared me.

I aimed the Taser downward.

"Or else you'll know what it feels like to get a Taser directly to the balls," I threatened.

Instead of backing off, he fucking laughed at me.

I growled back at him. He needed to take me seriously. I was going to make sure he did. I pulled in my core and carefully aimed at him, taking his hard cock and his balls right into my line of sight. He was going to pay for that.

My pussy clenched hard as I stared at him and I tried to remain as focused as I could, even if his nakedness was both thoroughly distracting and embarrassingly arousing at the same time.

I was a pretty good shot with a gun. I'd probably be pretty good with this. It wasn't like I was packing a heavy 9mm bullet in this thing.

I readied myself. Then he stepped forward toward me and I simply reacted on instinct.

I pulled that trigger.

The tiny darts shot forward, arcing until they connected

straight into his balls and he grunted with pain. A thin wire remained attached to my gun and when I pulled the trigger a second time, electricity propelled straight into his most sensitive place without a moment's delay.

He pitched forward and I was delighted to hear his high-pitched cry of pain as a result. One knee fell to the ground followed by the other as he crumpled in agony, cupping his hands around his balls as a terrible electric current coursed through his body. He'd left me no choice and I didn't give him any mercy as I flung the gun aside and decided to make my escape right then and there.

I turned and ran, using his downfall to my advantage. I sprinted hard and fast down the trail, following it until it forked. I took the left-hand path and dashed into the heavily wooded area, feeling twigs slap at my arms and branches snap against my face. I lifted a single arm and blocked their assault, although it still hurt all the same. I put everything into that escape because I needed to.

I don't know why, but my heart fell as I ran. I said goodbye to him and in my haste, I hardly noticed as a single tear rolled down my cheek. I ignored it, unsure of what it meant and continued to run until the path started to narrow. After that, the trail abruptly ended.

Instead of just standing there, I made my way off the trail and into the deeper brush. When I'd gone far enough, I found a tree with a branch about my height that I could reach, and I started to climb.

I was a really good climber. I'd trained on the walls at my gym for a long time and I'd taken a number of long weekend trips to the country into order to ascend more challenging cliffs and outcroppings. I liked to take pictures at the very top of my climbs and my office back at the university had several of my favorites beautifully framed and hung on my walls. They reminded me of my freedom when I was locked inside my office and reading yet another densely worded grant proposal.

I finally paused to catch my breath, looking out across the trees and seeing the mountains rising all above us. I'd never climbed out here before and it was astonishingly picturesque to behold. I sat on the branch and pressed my back against the trunk of the tree, dangling my legs to either side. My inner thighs squeezed around the branch and held me securely in place, ensuring I didn't fall to the ground to my death. I looked down and figured I was at least twenty to twenty-five feet in the air, which didn't particularly bother me. In fact, I kind of liked it. It felt safe.

For a while, all was silent. I allowed myself to relax, carefully stretching sore muscles. Then I heard a growl from down below and I sighed with disappointment. It hadn't been enough. I didn't even have to look because instinctually I already knew it was him waiting for me to come to him.

I did look down though, even though I didn't want to.

A strange tremor of fear and relief passed through me at the sight of him.

He was human once more and still entirely too naked.

"Omega, although I'm impressed with your feisty nature and the fact that your aim was true to your word, once I catch you, you're going to have to make it up to me. You're going to soothe the spot you just tased. And you're going to be doing it with your tongue," he warned gently, all while a small smirk curved up at the corners of his lips. He remained calm and that made me fear him all the more. He should be angry and mean, not amused and fascinated by my defiance. It left me feeling unbalanced and uncertain, which turned me on all the same.

I could feel myself growing wet once more.

"If you don't come down, you're going to regret it very

much when I climb up there and get you," he said, all the while keeping his contemplative and all too composed tone.

"I won't do it," I snarled.

His upper lip rolled at my challenge and I was suddenly reminded of a feral creature. My pussy tightened with need. I ignored it.

"You see, little mate, the only thing that's up to you now is if you're going to be doing it after a spanking or after a very thorough switching. Then maybe you'll understand the proper order between me and you," he warned, and I shivered at his threat. How dare he? He wasn't going to lay a single hand on me. I wouldn't allow it.

"That is never going to happen," I shot back. Over my fucking dead body.

He chuckled in amusement. I wanted to think him a rabid creature, a wild beast that answered to no one but himself. I wanted to think he was dangerous and violent, but he was too calm, too level-headed and that was doing very funny things to my insides that I was too ashamed to admit. I licked my lips and closed my eyes, afraid of what that might mean. I didn't want to understand it, but I was fearful that I would soon.

"You see, little mate, your place is by my side. It isn't up to you whether you want to be or not because fate has decreed that you are mine. After this is all over today, you will know what that means very, very thoroughly. See, you fight me, but I am faster, stronger, and I know a great many ways to subdue you and show you that you will only ever be mine. Sometimes those ways will hurt. Sometimes they will bring you pleasure. Most oftentimes though, those ways will bring you both," he said, and I trembled with fear and arousal.

I wanted to believe him. I was ashamed that I did.

"I don't want this. I didn't ask for any of this," I whispered.

I wanted to hate him. I wanted to run and escape but with every word he uttered, I could feel my body heat with desire. I wanted him badly and I hated myself for it.

"None of us has asked for our fates, but it is up to us to make the best of it with the paths we are given," he answered calmly.

I looked away, ignoring his words.

"Come down to me, little mate, and your punishment will be less severe," he said gently. I shook my head. I couldn't give in. It wasn't in my nature.

"No, I won't do it," I answered.

He licked his lips and his eyes darkened considerably. He smiled, but it felt dangerous and it carried with it a sense of ominous foreboding that left me fearfully anxious.

"That's alright, little mate. I'm glad you refused because when I do finally catch you, I'm very much going to enjoy switching that beautifully naked bottom of yours. I'm really going to enjoy seeing my mark on your pretty bare skin as I teach you what your rightful place really means," he threatened.

I gritted my teeth.

"You wouldn't dare," I exclaimed, staring down at him with open challenge.

"Oh, I would. I really would," he answered quietly, his tone menacing.

He circled the trunk of the tree, all the while keeping his gaze up on me.

"You see, sometimes a defiant mate needs to be reminded that there is a power structure and a hierarchy between a bonded pair. An omega always answers to her alpha and if she doesn't, she is thoroughly punished until she learns that she must obey. I'm going to teach you that lesson today," he continued.

"Fuck you," I interrupted, and his face never even

remotely twitched in either irritation or rage. It was strangely unnerving.

"Let me tell you what is going to happen. When I catch you, I'm going to strip you of every single piece of clothing until you are entirely bare before me because I find that feisty little mates are not so feisty once they are completely naked and properly presented for punishment. Then I'm going to take you over my knee and spank your disobedient little backside until you beg me to stop, but I'm not going to. You see, you're also going to learn today that when a punishment will end is not up to you. It's up to me and you're going to be spanked until there are tears dripping down your cheeks because I'm not going to stop until you're sobbing. Do you think it'll end there, my omega?"

"Yes." I whispered, fearful that it wouldn't.

I couldn't stop the desire from welling inside me. I should hate the fact that he was threatening me with a spanking, a punishment intended for naughty little girls. I'd never been chastised like that before, but right now my pussy was tightening with excitement. I was also soaking wet. I could feel it in the seat of my panties, and I was so ashamed of reacting to him like this. I didn't want it. It couldn't be real.

But it was. It was so very real.

The more he talked about what was about to happen, the more I began to trust that he wasn't some rabid monster. Sadistic maybe, but he continued to remain calm. He didn't appear to be angry or annoyed that I'd used a Taser on him and shot him straight in the balls, which any other man would be rightfully furious and far less put together than he was right now.

Not him though. This man was very different.

"That's where you're wrong, sweet mate. That's when the real punishment is going to begin. When I've finished your spanking, I'm going to help you up and then you're going to pick out your very own switch so that I can use it to thoroughly mark your disobedient little bottom until I'm certain that you've learned your lesson. I'm going to warn you though, if I'm not pleased with your choice, I will pick a switch myself and I will use it on your defiant naked backside until it breaks and then I'll give you the chance to choose another one. Does this make you fear me, little mate?" he asked.

"Yes," I whispered. My clit was throbbing with intense need and I tried to ignore it despite how aroused I was becoming as he told me what he had planned for me.

"Good," he answered.

It was obvious now that he wasn't some feral beast out to really hurt me. It didn't appear like I was in danger of being killed or maimed in any way. Instead, he'd thought through his words and presented me with what he thought was right in his world even though it was not in mine. It felt like I was running out of options and a painful introduction to his ways was becoming more and more likely with every passing moment.

I was afraid, just like he'd asked, but I was also incredibly aroused. I swallowed, trying to push every ounce of desire away. As much as I tried though, I was fighting a losing battle. Fear pulsed through me, but so did a very intense need to feel his touch. His threat of punishment left me feeling aroused and curious and so very, very wet. It was hard not to touch myself, to not drift my fingers over my breasts or between my legs. It was even becoming difficult to breathe and I found myself panting quietly as the heat simmered within me.

I felt hot, unbelievably hot. It was as though a fever had taken a hold of me and the only thing that I wanted to do was to take off my clothes and jump into a cool pool of water in order to chase it away. I licked my lips, unable to tear my eyes away from his cock for a long moment.

I stared at him from above in the tree, at least twenty feet above him, and his blue eyes met mine. They remained confident, but still remarkably soothing in the same breath.

"If you don't come down, or if you do and decide to run, little mate, I will catch you and your naked bottom isn't going to be the only place that gets switched today," he warned cautiously.

I didn't even want to think about what that might mean. I sat up on the branch that had been my resting place for several seconds longer, while I glowered down at him. Would he really spank me? Did I want to test him? Did I really want to see what would happen if I did?

I had to decide if I was ready to find out what a spanking felt like.

I wasn't naïve enough to think that he wouldn't climb the tree to come get me if I didn't climb down. Even if he didn't, I'd have to come down eventually. I couldn't sleep up here. It would be far too dangerous because I had no way of securing myself to the tree to keep from falling. It was a long way down and if I did fall, it would ultimately be the end of me.

I had zero doubts in my mind that he wouldn't allow that.

I no longer had any weapons to protect me. I'd dropped the Taser while climbing up to my current perch, but now I was stuck here in a tree and I had nowhere else to go but down to him.

I looked around me, trying to figure out if there were any other avenues available to me. None of the branches in my reach appeared to be particularly strong. The one I was currently sitting on was probably the thickest and the strongest one at this height. I couldn't travel along the trees far above him. That escape path was not an option either.

There was little choice left for me. I had to climb down.

"Come down to me, little mate, and I will ensure that you're rewarded in the end," he said, his voice just as soothing as it had been before. It made me want to come to him.

I gritted my teeth. I wasn't going to give in that easily.

Carefully, I climbed down the tree. Painfully slowly, I made sure each foothold and hand hold was secure before I descended and eventually, I made it all the way to the ground. I turned to face the man who had come for me and he held out his hand, fully expecting me to come to him for whatever punishment he planned to give me.

I didn't plan on getting spanked today though.

I bolted in the other direction and I heard him chuckle behind me in amusement.

"You're going to regret this very much in just a little while, omega," he murmured under his breath. I ignored him as I ran away.

My feet crashed into the ground, the dead twigs and dying leaves beneath my feet crunching as I tore away. I heard him behind me, his footsteps gaining closer and closer, and I ran even harder.

It wasn't enough. His hand clasped around my upper arm and he ground to a halt, bringing me to a complete stop with him. I swung around and tried to land a punch straight to his throat, but his fist caught mine in midair and forced it down. I whimpered as he bent my wrist backwards just enough to warn me that he could actually hurt me if he wanted to until I gave in to him, relaxing my arm in the process.

"I think you're not going to particularly enjoy what happens next, little mate, but rest assured, I certainly will," he threatened gently.

I clenched my teeth.

"Don't do this. I'm not the one you're looking for. I'm

only human," I said brazenly. Right now, I'd say anything just to get away from him.

"My omega is supposed to be human. Your fate is written deep within your soul and it ties you to me. Tell me, don't you feel it?" he asked before he pulled me into his arms and tenderly traced his fingers over the cusp of my right breast.

My pussy clamped down tight and my nipples tightened into sensitive little peaks beneath the protective layers of my clothing.

"You're a monster," I exclaimed, nervously trying to figure out how to escape his secure grasp. I soon realized that it wasn't possible.

"Don't lie to me, omega. You do not think of me in that way," he murmured as he pressed a soft kiss to the side of my temple. His touch was surprisingly tender, and I had to remind myself not to melt into his gentleness when he had already threatened such harsh retribution just minutes ago.

I knew he was right. I didn't think of him as a monster. He was a mystery to me, a terrifying beast that could shift into a wild animal at a moment's notice, but he was also a man capable of curling his arms around me and as much as his threats of punishment made me fear him, I felt a desire to find out more about him. I was also anxiously aroused for what came next.

I had a feeling I would soon find out.

"You won't hurt me?" I ventured. I had to know. I wanted to know what he had in store for me.

"Your punishment is going to hurt, little mate, because I think that you need it to. But after it's all over, I'm going to show you what it truly means to belong to an alpha. Even now, I know you want it. I can smell just how wet you are for me. Even though you know you're about to go over my knee for a very hard spanking, you're soaked, and you can't hide it from me, even though you're fully clothed. Does that make you even wetter for me, my little mate?"

I keened with surprise. His far superior sense of smell had picked up on my dirty little secret. I blushed with shame even as he chuckled knowingly at his discovery.

He pressed the hard length of his cock against my ass and I gasped at the feeling of it. It made me feel wanted. It made me feel special. It made me want him even more.

"Do you feel that? Do you feel how hard I am when I think about how I'm going to take you over my knee, spank your naughty bottom until you're sobbing, and then truly teach you your place at the end of a switch?" he warned. His voice shook with his own desire and a quiet moan escaped my lips at his dangerous threats.

I shivered with need.

"Don't," I replied.

"It's no longer up to you, little omega. It's about time you learned just that," he whispered into my ear, his breath tickling the tiny hairs along my skin. His cock felt impossibly hard against me and all I wanted was to feel his thick length between my thighs. I needed him to fuck me.

I was used to having control. I was used to leading my own team, but I had the very distinct feeling that I was going to find out how very much I was out of my element very soon.

"I don't even know your name," I exclaimed anxiously, all while battling the rampant desire pulsing between my legs.

"My name is Kiba. Will you tell me yours, little mate?" he asked, and I found myself wanting to answer him.

"Dawn," I whispered softly, and his answering groan was so arousing that it almost brought me to my knees. He grasped my chin and turned my face toward his before he captured me in a kiss that devastated me in a matter of seconds. He claimed me hard in that first embrace and I found myself melting into his arms. I kissed him back with fervor, despite the fact that I was so very reluctant to give into him. When he finally pulled away, it had left me breathless and unsteady. I was thankful for his strength in that moment.

"It's nice to meet you, Dawn. I look forward to learning more about you, but I think it's time you took your rightful place over my knee and learned what happens to naughty little mates who disobey their alphas," he murmured, and I stiffened. I would have tried to run again, but there was nowhere to go, and his arms held me tight. He was faster than me. He was stronger and there was nothing I could do to keep myself out of his reach. I knew that now. Whatever was to happen next felt like it was inevitable, as if it was fate.

His hands squeezed tight around my shoulders and then, he moved quickly before I had a chance to run again. He unwrapped himself from my body and swiftly grasped the collar of my shirt before he ripped it open, popping the buttons off in a matter of seconds. Shocked, I watched them fall to the forest floor beneath my feet. He shredded my shirt right off my back, taking it and tearing it into strips with ease. I watched him nervously, resigned to the fact that I was at this beast's mercy until someone came for me. That is, if anyone came to rescue me, but I had a feeling no one was coming.

He grabbed the flimsy material of my bra and ripped it in half. My bra fell open, baring my breasts and I moved my hands to cover myself, embarrassingly ashamed of being exposed in such a barbaric fashion. He quickly knocked my hands away, growling in warning. I pressed my hands to my naked belly nervously, taking his threat to heart.

If I did it again, I would surely regret it.

Next, he unbuttoned and unzipped my jeans, sliding them slowly over my hips almost as if he was sending a message that he could do whatever he wanted with me. He pushed them down to my knees before he tore them from my body in a feat of strength only a man of his kind could be capable of. I whimpered nervously, standing before him now in only my panties and my hiking boots.

I'd never been stripped like this. He was tearing my clothes from my body and throwing them aside as if they were nothing just sheets of paper.

It was terrifying. It was arousing. It was all that and more.

"Don't," I tried to say.

"It's not up to you anymore, little omega. It's up to me, as your alpha," he answered. I trembled before him and he caressed my breast gently before sliding his fingers down my belly and cupping between my thighs.

"You protest, but your little pussy is telling me what you need. You're so wet that I can smell you and now I can feel it against my palm. You want this and as much as you try to deny it, you need your alpha to put you in your place. You need me to punish you, don't you, little mate?"

He wanted me to answer. I couldn't give it to him.

His fingers traced along the hem of my lacey blue underwear, teasing me with his soft touch. Without thinking, I just reacted, and my hips curled forward toward him.

I wondered what his fingers would feel like as they touched the place I so desperately wanted to be touched, what they would feel like as they pressed deep into my pussy. Fuck. I wanted him to take me and I hated that I did.

I was so aroused. I'd never felt this turned on in my life. This was wrong. I shouldn't be reacting like this, but I couldn't make it stop.

His fingers grazed over my mound, finding my clit and circling gently over top of it. He teased and taunted me until I was breathless with need and then he slipped his hand beneath the lacey fabric of my panties, gripped and tore it from my body in one brutally hard motion. I cried out as the fabric pinched at my wet folds. It hurt and I whimpered from the painful bite. I tried to press my fingers in between my legs. He didn't let me.

Instead, he placed his finger there in my place. Carefully, he pressed against my wet channel, but he didn't enter me. He just held it there instead, a firm reminder that he could do as he pleased with me and I had no power to stop it from happening.

"Such a very wet little pussy. I think you want me to punish you, don't you, little mate," he murmured, and I rocked my hips against him, trying to give myself relief but he pulled his hand away and I found none.

Unexpectedly, he curled those wet fingers around my wrist as he sat down on a nearby boulder. Before I even had a moment to stop what was happening, he jerked me forward and I fell over his thighs, completely naked and vulnerable to whatever he had planned for me.

Fuck.

I tried so hard to get away so this wouldn't take place, but now it was happening anyway. I attempted to push myself up and his hand curled around my hips, pressing down firmly and holding me in place. All of my efforts to squirm and break out of his grasp were thwarted and I found myself drumming my toes against the ground in defeat. He chuckled and pressed his palm carefully against my bottom before he glided it over top of my bare flesh.

I stilled, suddenly far more nervous than before.

His fingers dipped between my thighs and slid along my wet folds. The direct contact of his skin on mine was humbling, thoroughly reminding me that I was helpless to whatever he wanted to do with me. His touch glided back and forth. I whimpered, with either pleasure or shock I didn't know. Without thinking, I arched my back and aided in his explorations. He found my naked clit and circled it, ensuring that he kept the pressure light enough to tease me into a mindless frenzy of need.

He continued taunting me, edging me closer and closer to orgasm until I thought I would break apart over his knees.

"This wet little pussy knows that your alpha is about to teach you a very first lesson. It knows to obey its master," he said quietly, and a tremor of pleasure quaked through my thighs. I was ashamed that he was right. I was soaking wet for him as I lay naked over his lap about to be spanked for the first time in my life.

His fingers abandoned my soaked pussy and I whined in disappointment. He'd left me on the edge of release and my core throbbed with need.

His palm returned to my naked backside.

"Can you feel how aroused I am when I'm about to spank you?" he asked, before he lightly slapped my right cheek, just jostling my bottom enough to make my pussy clench down hard.

I could feel it. His hard cock was pressing into my hip and I wanted nothing more than for him to lift me up and sit me down right on top of it.

But I wasn't going to get that. I had a punishment coming first.

He lightly smacked my ass once again and I lifted my hips, an invitation for his fingers to make their return to my needy little pussy. They didn't and I pouted with disappointment.

Instead, they roughly squeezed the flesh of my bottom before his palm spanked me hard for the very first time. My mouth opened wide in shock as the sound echoed all around me, bouncing off the trees deafeningly loud and so very shamefully. Anyone nearby would be able to hear what was happening and know that I was getting punished in the way that naughty little girls were meant to be punished. He spanked me again and I squeaked in surprise as the sting came over me for the first time.

Fuck. It hurt quite a bit more than I expected. His palm was broad and as he spanked me, the area of it encompassed much of the entirety of my backside. He slapped each cheek hard after that and I tried to kick and escape it, but his aim proved to be true each time. I whimpered loudly as the full realization of how very unprepared I was to be spanked by him.

"You don't have to do this, Kiba!" I exclaimed, trying one more time to appeal to his senses and stop the spanking before it went too far.

"I really think I do," he answered and then the spanking truly began.

His palm crashed down into my naked bottom much harder than before, over and over again until I was sure that he'd painted my whole backside red. He didn't miss a single inch as he paddled from the tops of my cheeks all the way down to the bottom curves of my ass, ensuring to spend extra time in the place where my thighs began.

"Stop!" I shrieked as the pain really started to build on itself. It felt like a thousand bees had stung me at once. My bottom was quickly becoming very sore and I just wanted it to end.

"Your punishment is far from over, little omega. You've earned a very thorough lesson and I'm going to ensure you remember every moment of it," he replied darkly, and a shiver of pleasure and fear raced down my spine. My core twisted hard with need.

Despite all of my protests, the spanking continued. His palm rained down on my bottom until I thought I couldn't take anymore. But I did. He was going to ensure that I took a whole lot more. I tried to hold in my cries. I tried to remain stoic and strong so that he didn't think me weak. Before long though, I was whimpering despite how hard I tried to stop it.

He spanked me hard, his punishment ruthless, or at least I thought it was until he started paddling my thighs.

If I had thought it had hurt as much as it could before, I had been wrong. Very wrong. His palm felt that much harsher on the backs of my legs, the terrible sting that much more intense. My cries got louder and more desperate and I started to beg.

"Please. Please, sir. Please don't," I pleaded. I don't know why I'd said those words. Nothing could take them back. Something about calling him sir felt right though and I tried not to think too much into it. I certainly didn't think about the fact that it made me even wetter as the words had escaped my mouth.

He ignored me. He continued to punish my bare bottom and my tender thighs with cruel precision and even as I tried to fight it, I could feel myself beginning to spiral out of control. My breath hitched in the back of my throat and I squeezed my eyes shut in an attempt to stop myself from crying. That only lasted so long.

Then he spanked me even harder.

I squirmed. I whimpered, and I tried everything I could to escape. I kicked and rolled my hips, yet nothing worked. His hand on my hip held me firmly against his thighs, ensuring that I stayed in my place as he spanked me very hard just like he'd said he would. I tried to reach back to cover my exposed backside. His forearm prevented it and I whined as I wrapped my fingers around his ankle, trying to get ahold of myself before I broke down completely.

"Please!" I begged. I was struggling not to cry and the tremor in my voice gave away just how very close I was. He'd be able to tell. There was no doubt in my mind.

The worst part of it all was that I knew how very wet this

was making me, how much more aroused I was than before this all started. I could feel the desire to come even more strongly. Liquid heat gathered between my thighs, so much so that I could feel it dripping down my legs. I was probably leaving a wet spot on his skin beneath me and I was so very ashamed that getting a spanking was having such an effect on me.

I shouldn't be getting turned on by this. I should be angry, furious even, but the only thing I wanted to do when he finally let me up was jump on his cock and ride it with everything in me. I craved it. I needed it and when this was all over, I sincerely hoped he would give it to me.

I knew he was just as turned on as I was. I could feel how hard his cock was against my hip. It was throbbing with his own need.

Fuck.

He slapped my thighs particularly hard then and it broke me out of my thoughts. He focused on them now entirely and my breath hitched once more.

It hurt. Fucking hell, it hurt so much.

I could feel myself losing control. After several more particularly merciless smacks against my thighs, the first unwilling tear escaped my eyes and rolled down my cheek. Followed by another. And another until I was openly sobbing over his knees.

Still, the spanking didn't end.

"Now, little mate, I think you're ready to begin accepting your place. What happens next is going to make sure that you remember it," he warned.

His palm paddled me quickly and more harshly than ever. I sobbed, unable to stop myself from crying as his hand cracked down on my very sore bottom over and over. It was as though a fire was blazing across my tender flesh and nothing was ever going to put it out. He spanked me hard and fast, a very clear message that I no longer made the rules. He did and he wouldn't hesitate to remind me of that whenever he deemed necessary. I accepted his painful punishment as tears rolled down my cheeks.

I finally gave in. I submitted to my alpha.

I cried hard. I pleaded my apologies and I promised to be a very good girl. The spanking began to slow, but each slap carried with it the weight of the world as they cracked against my naked backside.

I sobbed even harder.

"I'm sorry for running from you, sir," I whispered, and I curled against him.

The spanking finally stopped.

"That's a very good girl. I'm proud of how well you took your very first spanking over my knees, little mate," he murmured, his voice gentle and soothing as I cried over his lap. He gathered me in his arms and held me against his chest. My bottom burned hotly as it pressed against his thighs, a constant reminder that this man had stripped me and put me over his knees for a very hard and painful spanking.

My tears dried as he held me, and then he cleared his throat.

CHAPTER 5

Dawn

I HAD A FEELING my ordeal was far from over and once he began to speak, I knew I was right.

"I'll never give you more than you can take, my sweet omega, but you earned a very thorough punishment and it isn't over yet. What happens next is going to ensure that you won't ever forget your place again. Now you're going to pick out three switches for me in three different lengths. The thickest and the longest one will be used to thoroughly switch your already sore little bottom. The medium length one will be used to punish your breasts and those delightfully pretty nipples. Then, after all that is over, I'll use the smallest one to switch that pretty little pussy until you promise me that you will be a good little omega who will always obey her alpha," he explained darkly.

My mouth went dry and I could have sworn my stomach

dropped straight to my toes. He wasn't serious. He couldn't be.

"Please," I begged. "I've learned my lesson."

"You're not the one who gets to decide that anymore, my beautiful omega. I've decided that your lesson needs to continue, and you don't have a choice about whether or not you're going to take it. It's not up to you. It's up to me," he replied firmly.

A soft whimper escaped my lips. I quivered with need. His words made me afraid, but they also did very strange things to my body. My breasts were heavy with desire, my nipples pebbled into tender little peaks at the prospect of feeling the merciless bite of a switch. My pussy tightened and my clit throbbed as I wondered it how very much was going to hurt to be switched there too.

I feared getting a switching, but it also made me wet knowing it was going to happen very soon whether I wanted it to or not. He'd decided that he was going to give me one and it didn't matter what I thought about it.

I'd never felt more out of control than I did now. He'd taken every ounce of it for himself. I didn't understand why that aroused me so much.

"Sir," I pleaded, hiding my face in his shoulder.

"Do you want another spanking before your switching, little mate?" he asked, his voice laced with a very real threat.

"No, sir," I answered quickly, feeling very small and vulnerable. There was no doubt in my mind now that he wouldn't follow through with what he said he would do. If he wanted to spank me again, he would.

"I don't know what to look for in a switch. I've never been switched before, sir," I said quietly, knowing that I was going to have to find several that pleased him very soon whether I liked it or not.

"The branch is not to be too thick, but slender and supple

so that it is flexible. Younger trees are best for this and yield a number of thin branches that would make good switches. Once you choose one, I will break it off for you. I will then remove the leaves and twigs stemming off of it. When you have chosen your three switches and I'm pleased with your choices, the rest of your punishment will begin," he explained.

My pussy clenched hard. As afraid as I was right now, I'd never wanted to orgasm so badly in my life.

He offered me a hand and I used it to stand on shaky legs. I met those icy blue eyes, finding them staring back at me with unmerciful firmness.

Reluctantly, I turned away and walked over to some nearby trees. I found a young sapling and ran my fingers along its wood, trying to figure out exactly what he was looking for. He had warned me before that if my choices didn't please him, he'd break one off himself and switch me so hard that it broke and then I'd have to choose another. This would happen again and again until he was happy with the switches that I'd picked, I had no doubt of that.

I swallowed nervously.

Something loud cracked behind me and I turned back to him. He'd taken two rocks in his hands and had smashed them together, creating some sort of makeshift blade that I assumed he'd used to trim the branches that were soon going to be whipping the very naked and most tender places on my body.

I started looking amongst the trees once more, trying to find the perfect one that would please him.

I found a thin branch as long as my arm and pointed it out to him. He walked over to join me and used his stone blade to cut it off. Anxiously, I watched him as he trimmed off the leaves and the smaller twigs until he had one single long switch. He placed it on top of a boulder nearby. It was rather ominous as it laid there, an innocent branch that was about to play a not so innocent role in the punishing of my already very sore backside.

"This is a good choice. It will mark your bottom nicely," he said, and I breathed a sigh of relief. I understood what he was looking for now.

I looked carefully and chose another that was about half the size of the first one. It was about the length of my forearm and a bit thinner. He grunted his approval, cutting that one and trimming it just as he'd done the other. When he was finished, he laid it beside the longer switch and I swallowed nervously as I thought about the fact that it was going to whip my breasts, as well as my nipples very soon.

"Time to choose the one that will punish that very pretty and very wet little pussy. This switch will hurt the most, sweet girl, but you're going to take it because it's exactly what you need," he said sternly, and I whimpered quietly. I pressed my legs together anxiously as if that would protect me from what was to come, and I couldn't help but notice that my inner thighs were soaked with my arousal.

I fidgeted nervously as I looked at the tree, feeling like I was being forced to play an active role in my very own doom. Having to choose each switch made the possibility of it actually happening very real, making me anticipate what each one would feel like as it whipped against my skin.

With even more reluctance, I reached for the shorter branches, feeling for the suppleness and flexibility that would be required in order to whip the place in between my thighs. A number were far too brittle, and I passed over them before I found one that was about half the length of the medium one that I'd already chosen. This one seemed so much worse though, since I knew it was going to switch the most sensitive spot on my body. I had a feeling it was going to make me cry and he was going to be able to see every last tear when it finally happened.

"This one, sir," I whispered, my mouth as dry as cotton.

He took it in his fingers and ran them down the length of the branch, testing it and flexing it back and forth before he purred his agreement. I would have sighed in relief that I'd chosen acceptable switches and that I wasn't going to be whipped with one until it broke, but it also meant that the rest of my punishment was going to happen far sooner than I was ready for. It was going to begin now.

He laid the third switch on the boulder by the others. I stared at it with extreme reluctance and tried to swallow away my unquenchable fear and ever-building desire.

Then he picked up what remained of my shirt and tossed it over a fallen log. Calmly, he extended his arm toward me and I tentatively took it, knowing that I had no other choice. With a gentleness I wasn't sure I deserved, he led me over to the log and laid me over top of it lengthwise. After that, he tore strips of cloth from what remained of my jeans. I waited, staying where he put me.

He returned to me and bound my hands together. He also tied a very long piece around my waist, securing me to the log. I wasn't able to roll or move off of it. I felt so very helpless and vulnerable bound this way and I was sure that he knew it too.

My pussy tightened with need and I whimpered softly, very nervous for what was to come. His fingers traced lightly up the backs of my thighs and I looked up at him with trepidation.

His cock was so very hard. He was enjoying punishing me like this.

He caught me staring and I blushed, forcing myself to turn away.

His fingers dipped in between my legs.

"So very, very wet, little mate. You protest, but this little pussy is telling me that this is exactly what you want," he said softly, and I whined with shame. He pressed one finger into my pussy, and I shuddered with pleasure.

"Please," I begged.

"Not yet, my pretty little omega. You've got quite a switching coming before I allow you to come all over my cock," he answered, his voice dark and dangerous and entirely too fuckable.

He strode over to the boulder and took the longest switch into his fingers. He swished it through the air and the sound made me shiver in fearful arousal.

"I gave you an instruction before, and you ignored it. This punishment is going to ensure that it won't happen again, isn't that right?"

"Yes, sir," I whimpered.

I felt so exposed. So vulnerable. I didn't feel even remotely feisty or defiant anymore.

Instead, I felt like a little girl who was about to find out what happened when she was very naughty and then got caught. I had a feeling I was about to understand what it truly meant to be punished. My spanking had only been the beginning.

"Please, I won't run again," I begged.

"I know," he replied. He laid the switch on my naked bottom.

"I'm sorry I tased you," I pleaded, hoping my words would stop what seemed so very inevitable right now.

"I know that too, little mate. You'll get your chance to soothe the place that you tased with your tongue after I've decided your beautiful little body has been punished to my satisfaction," he said firmly, and my core twisted hard.

He wanted to fuck my mouth. I was sure of it.

"Please, I've learned my lesson," I begged. "You don't need to switch me."

"Of the two of us, who gets to choose how you are punished?" he pressed.

"You do, sir," I answered timidly. My legs flexed nervously as the switch laid against my already sore backside and I nervously awaited its cruel bite.

"That's correct. I'm going to enjoy switching your beautifully bare bottom, your pretty breasts, and your wet little pussy. You're going to scream and beg and you're going to cry for me, but your punishment is only going to end when I've decided you've had enough. Is that clear, little girl?"

"Yes, sir," I whispered. I could hardly breathe, I was so nervous. My legs quivered with fear and my inner walls fluttered as liquid heat gathered between my thighs.

I heard the switch cut through the air and my entire body tensed as I waited for its fall. Once it whipped against my freshly spanked skin, the resulting sting was swift and overwhelming and painfully brutal. My chest rose and fell as I struggled to take that single lash and when I finally began to calm, he switched me again.

The resulting crescendo of pain built on the first and I did everything I could to remain stoic and strong, but the line of fire was so much harsher than I was prepared for. He switched me for a third time, and I couldn't stop myself as I wailed in response to its painful lash.

Fuck. It hurt so very, very much.

He took his time switching me, ensuring that I experienced each moment of the branch's cruel sting. Sometimes, he would pause and walk around me, showing me that his cock was impossibly hard. It was obvious that he very much liked punishing me this way. My pussy ached to be full of that very hard cock.

Without warning, he whipped me hard and fast with that long, slender switch.

I wailed from the agonizing sting as I felt the welts rise up on my skin. My entire bottom blazed with fire and I sniffed back my tears, trying to hold myself together but it was so very difficult.

"I'm enjoying seeing my marks on your beautiful bottom, little omega," he said softly, and my eyes flicked up to look at his cock once more. It stood high and gloriously erect and I wanted it inside me so very badly.

The switch was ruthless, and I hated every cruel bite despite the fact that I could feel how very wet it was making me. Each welt burned like a blistering brand that seared into my sore flesh. I could feel each one rising, the scalding pain building as the seconds crept by after each fateful lash.

This was a very hard lesson, one I was struggling to take.

I squeezed my eyes shut and folded my hands together. There was no way for me to reach back because of the way he'd restrained me. I couldn't roll to avoid the switch either, bound as I was to the fallen log. There was no choice left for me except to take what he gave me, and I soon wondered how much that would be.

Then he started to whip the backs of my thighs.

Almost immediately, I choked back a sob. When the second painful lash fell against my thighs, I wailed and I began to beg. Not long after that, I started to cry. I told him how very sorry I was, how I would never defy him again and if he would please consider my lesson over. I asked for his mercy. I begged him for it.

"Please, let me make it up to you. Please let me suck your cock. I'll do anything. Please," I pleaded through my tears. I sobbed openly. I no longer cared how shameful the words coming out of my mouth were. I only wanted the switching to stop.

"Don't worry, little omega. You'll do all that and more after your switching is over," he assured me, and I wailed in defeat. Nothing I did or said would convince him to stop. I understood that completely now.

The absolute power he had over me was in stark contrast to my complete lack of it. He'd taken thorough control of me because he was my alpha, and because I was his to control.

Even as I cried, my pussy throbbed with need, calling for him to claim me in the way I was meant to be taken.

He switched me another five times in quick succession and I sobbed hard. I hardly noticed when he'd placed the cruel switch back on the boulder. Then he returned to me and untied the clothing around my waist. After that, he freed my wrists and I was able to unwind my arms from around the log.

"Come. Stand here," he instructed. I sniffed back my tears and obeyed, too fearful to even think about being disobedient. He tossed the long piece of fabric over a strong branch above me and proceeded to lift my arms over my head. He bound my wrists with that same strip of cloth.

"I want you to test it. Put all of your weight into your wrists and suspend yourself in the air," he directed. Obediently, I pulled myself up by the strength of my arms so that my feet left the forest floor. The branch and the restraints held my weight with ease. He purred his approval and my nipples pebbled with desire.

Next, he spread my legs apart and bound each of my ankles to two nearby saplings. My legs felt spread obscenely wide and I whimpered, realizing how much I was on display for him. I tried to bring my thighs together and hide the wetness I knew was practically dripping from me, but I couldn't. His restraints prevented that.

My punished backside ached, the residual smolder from the welts left by the switch still burning hot. I ached to touch them and soothe the painful marks, but bound as I was, I knew I wouldn't be able to for some time.

He didn't pick up that medium length switch right away. Instead, he stood before me and admired my naked form, taking his time to let his eyes drift up and down so that he could see absolutely everything. He circled me and I'd never felt more like a lamb left out to slaughter than I did at that moment. His fingers glided down my back and onto my bottom, tracing the welts he'd left behind.

"It gives me great pride to see my mark on your beautiful skin. Your bottom is so very pretty when it's properly reddened and welted to my satisfaction," he murmured, and a shudder of desire raced down my spine and pooled between my thighs.

His touch skated along my flesh, circling my hips and smoothing across my stomach until he lifted my right breast in his palm. He grazed his thumb over top of my nipple, causing it to harden under his touch. Gently, he pinched it between two fingers and a moan of desire managed to escape my lips. He smiled knowingly and he lifted his other hand to capture my left breast too.

He teased my nipples, pinching them softly and making them pebble under his skillful touch. Gradually, the pinches grew harder, the twists rougher and I tried to turn my body in order to break his hold. Instead, he took each nipple firmly between his fingertips and lifted my breasts with them. I whimpered, feeling how very heavy they felt with desire and then he pulled them away from me.

I whimpered because it started to hurt. His fingers squeezed and twisted harder. He punished my nipples until I couldn't stop myself from crying out, pain lancing across my breasts. When he finally released them, I bit my lower lip as a second wave of hurt followed the first.

Then, using his hand, he began to spank my breasts. I

whined in alarm as they jiggled shamefully but as he slapped them a bit harder, I no longer cared what they looked like. I was only concerned with the fact that it stung. Over and over he slapped each one, ensuring that he covered the entirety of my vulnerable and tender flesh. He didn't stop until my skin was bright pink and I was once again whimpering for his mercy. After that, he returned to punish my nipples, pinching them hard enough that I knew they would remain sore long after he released them. When he was finished, he slipped his hand in between my thighs.

"You're soaking wet, mate," he said loudly, and I shivered with shame. He coated two fingers with my wetness and removed them from my pussy, only to press them against my lips.

"Open. You're going to clean these off for me," he instructed.

I obeyed and opened my mouth. He pressed his fingers in between my lips and onto my tongue. My own sweet musky flavor surprised me. I didn't hate it, but it felt so shamefully wrong to be made to taste my own arousal like this. Tentatively, I began to cleanse his fingers with my mouth. I did the best that I could, ensuring to swirl my tongue around his digits until the taste of myself gradually faded away.

"Good girl," he murmured softly, and I could have sworn my heart leapt in my chest. I found myself suddenly wanting to hear those words fall from his lips again.

"Are your nipples sore now, little mate?" he asked.

"Yes, sir," I answered. Perhaps he'd decided I'd earned his sympathy.

"Good," he replied, before he turned around and lifted the medium switch up off the nearby bolder.

"Such pretty pink nipples you have, little mate. It becomes you to have your beautiful breasts spanked bright pink to match them," he said, carefully admiring his work. I couldn't help but notice the incredible hardness of his enormous cock and my pussy clenched down hard with need.

Carefully, he laid the switch against my breasts. He took his time to line it up with the peak of my left nipple and I trembled as I waited for what I imagined would be far more painful than being switched across my bottom.

His hand hardly moved as he flicked his wrist, so briefly that I almost didn't notice. The result of that motion though was agony. The tip of the switch whipped directly against my nipple and the terrible pain that seared across my breast was far worse than I'd imagined it to be. He repeated the same treatment on my right nipple, and it was that much crueler because now I knew exactly what was coming.

I wailed and the switch punished my breasts next, talking care to welt more of my chest than just my poor little nipples. My cries only seemed to encourage him. They even appeared to make his cock even harder than before.

"Please, sir," I begged. Even my own voice sounded desperate to my ears.

None of my words even made him hesitate for even a moment and my needy pussy clamped down hard as a result. He'd decided I'd needed to be punished and taught my place. I was just beginning to really understand what that meant now.

If I looked down at my punished breasts, I could see each welt from the switch rising on my pinkened skin. He slowly and methodically whipped me, making sure that no spot was left unmarked. He spent a great deal of time thrashing my nipples and I soon found myself fighting back tears once more. Occasionally, he'd stop and touch the welts he'd left behind, gently sliding his fingertips against my breasts and my nipples. I lived for those moments even though even just the slightest touch was painful because his tenderness starkly contrasted with his cruelty. He allowed me several moments to compose myself before the next lash fell and I was grateful for that.

"There isn't an inch of this beautiful little body that isn't mine now. If I want to pleasure you or punish you, I will do as I please," he said softly, and I felt his words down deep in the pit of my soul. It resonated within me and strangely enough, it made me feel alive. At the same time, it also made me feel free.

The switch whipped at each of my nipples in quick succession, but for the first time, I welcomed the subsequent sting of agony. Pleasure pooled between my thighs and I ached for him to touch me.

"Please," I begged. I wanted to come. I wanted him to fuck me.

His lips descended onto my nipple and his teeth carefully grazed against the tip. I arched into that sultry kiss and my pussy clamped down hard as his fingers drifted up my thighs. I wanted them inside me so badly. I wanted to feel them caressing my inner walls. I moaned softly and he kissed my other nipple. I didn't even care that they were sore. It made me want him all the more.

"I need…" I began.

"I know what you need, sweet mate," he whispered in return.

"Please," I pleaded.

"Not yet. There's one last place on this perfect little body that needs to be punished, isn't there?"

"Yes, sir," I wailed. My gaze returned to the boulder where the last of the switches lay unused. I could scarcely breathe as I watched him walk over to it and curl his fingers around that slender piece of wood. Slowly, he strode back to me and cocked his head to the side, assessing the way I couldn't catch my breath. My heart pounded in my chest and I wondered if he could hear it.

"The air is scented heavily with that sweet little pussy. You're so much wetter knowing that you're about to be punished there too, aren't you, little omega?"

I wished I could turn my head. I wished he'd stop looking. Restrained with my arms high over my head, I couldn't even use my hair to shield my mortification. He could see everything, and my very last shred of dignity fell away. I couldn't hide a single tear or the way he was making me blush right now. I couldn't even conceal the fact that I knew he was right.

"Say it," he demanded, and I felt his command deep in my bones.

"Yes, sir," I moaned, too overcome with shame. He'd stripped my clothes and bared me, but I hadn't felt truly naked until this very moment. He'd exposed me utterly and completely and I discovered something about myself that I hadn't known existed.

The switch caressed the tender skin of my thighs, drifting upward until it just brushed against my wet folds. I sucked in an anxious breath, unable to control just how much my core was twisting and turning in anticipation.

He flicked his wrist and the switch connected with the sensitive flesh between my thighs. I keened, overcome with a sharp streak of agony. Two more followed in quick succession and I felt myself beginning to panic. My cries carried with them a certain sense of desperation and I begged him to allow me to make it up to him.

"Shh, sweet mate. I wouldn't ever give you more than you can take," he whispered tenderly and the panic inside me faded away. His fingers drifted between my thighs, caressing the little welts he'd left behind with the smallest switch. He paused and teased my clit with his fingertip before he pulled away and pressed the slender branch back in its place.

My chest rose and fell with anxious arousal. His eyes met

mine and I saw darkness and undeniable power within them. I felt so very small and so vulnerable there before him.

"Eyes on me, little omega. You're not allowed to hide from me ever again," he said dangerously, and I didn't dare disobey him.

The switch flicked upward and he was able to watch every minute change in my expression as the agonizing bite tore through me. My mouth opened into a round 'O' and my eyes watered. That wasn't all though.

I moaned.

I should hate having my pussy switched. I couldn't. Not when it happened like this. He growled softly in return and I ached for him.

He'd been harsh and quick to punish me, but he was fair. He'd given me plenty of warning that I was pushing him and when I'd continue to defy him, he'd showed me what would happen when he finally caught up with me. He'd stripped me, spanked me, and now he was showing me that my bottom wasn't the only place he could punish. My ass ached. My breasts and my nipples hummed with pain and now my pussy was next up to pay the price.

I was soaking wet. So wet that it was dripping down my thighs. I already knew he could smell it but now I was sure that he could see it too.

He kissed me firmly and at the same time, the switch thrashed my pussy hard and fast. I screamed but he swallowed the sound with that ravenous kiss. When he finally pulled away, I was left gasping as my wet folds stung hotly from his lash.

He teased me with it with the switch, coating the hard edge with my wetness. I groaned with pleasure as it rubbed against my clit and it took everything in me not to grind myself on top of it. I wanted to come so badly. My core twisted hard and I whimpered in pain, needing release like I needed air to breathe.

"Such a needy, desperate little omega," he said darkly, and I keened with arousal.

He switched my pussy with ruthless efficiency, taking care to welt every inch of me. I screamed and cried, and he paused once more to taunt me with that skinny piece of wood until all I wanted was his cock to take its place. He teased me until I thought I couldn't take anymore without falling apart.

My legs shook from the effort to hold myself up. My sore nipples pebbled hard with desire and I moaned, trying to show him with my body how very much I wanted him right now. My clit felt so desperately sensitive. I really needed to come, and soon.

Carefully, he reached between my thighs. I moaned again, thinking he was going to reward me now, but as he used two fingers to spread the lips of my pussy far apart, I realized I had been wrong. Through his careful movements, my clit was entirely exposed, and I stilled as he gently tapped the switch against it.

No. Please. He couldn't mean to.

"When I told you that there wasn't a single inch of your body that I wouldn't punish, I was very serious, little omega," he said sternly. I trembled hard, fearful and aroused and so very needy.

"Please don't," I begged. A single tear of desperation rolled down my cheek and he used his thumb to brush it away.

He didn't answer me with his words. Instead, he answered with the switch.

A fiery crescendo of agony burst across my clit and spread through my pussy, sinking down deep into my core. I sobbed openly as the overwhelming pain took over my senses. My legs gave way beneath me and he was there to catch me, using his strength to hold me up as I processed that final terrible stroke.

"Good girl," he murmured, saying the words over and over and I held onto them like a lifeline. With one arm supporting me, he quickly unbound me and gathered me against his chest. He swept the other switches off the boulder and placed me facedown over top of it. Gently, he guided my thighs apart and inspected my pussy, taking care to lightly touch the welts he'd left behind.

Everything hurt. My pussy was sore. My breasts ached and my nipples pulsed with residual pain. My bottom still burned from both his palm and the switch.

But then, his cock pressed up against my well-spanked pussy and I forgot how much his punishment had hurt. Now the only thing on my mind was how it would feel when he fucked me with his marvelously hard cock.

No longer bound, I lifted my hips in encouragement. He slid his hips back and forth, dragging his cock through my wetness and teasing my clit once more.

"Would you like to come for me, omega?"

"Yes, sir," I pleaded so very desperately.

I wanted to give him all of me. More than that though, I wanted him to take it.

The head of his cock brushed against my entrance, taunting me with its wide girth and I trembled with need.

"Please, give me your cock, sir," I begged, feeling myself blush as the filthy plea fell off my lips.

"Do you really want it, omega? Do you feel like you've earn the privilege of my cock?" he asked, and a jolt of intense pleasure raced straight to my core at those decadently dirty words. I panted with need, unabashed as I rocked my hips back and forth in an effort to show him how much I wanted him.

"Yes, sir," I answered, hoping against hope that he thought

I deserved it too. I was so weak with arousal that I wasn't sure how much more I was physically capable of taking. My clit pulsed, still feeling the painful sting from the switch and my pussy tightened hard, imagining what it would be like to feel his cock sliding inside me for the very first time.

I didn't have to wait long.

The moment that the head of his cock pressed into my tight channel, I keened with pleasure. He was huge and his entry hurt, but I didn't care because it was exactly what I wanted right now. I'd been punished so harshly and now I wanted to be rewarded with an orgasm so very badly. Most of all, I wanted to come all over his cock as he fucked me just as hard as I needed to be fucked.

His girth stretched my sore pussy wide as he forced himself into my entrance. I cried out, pain and pleasure combining into one intoxicating sensation that threatened to consume me whole. My inner walls clenched around his length with greed. His advance into me was slow and strong, a quiet lesson that he could take me however he wanted and whenever he wished. I could feel myself tightening around him, grasping at every enormous inch until he was fully seated inside me.

He remained motionless for several seconds and I whined with disappointment.

"Do you feel in control right now, omega?"

"No, sir," I whimpered.

"What did you learn today, my sweet omega?"

"That I'm yours. That you're my alpha, sir," I answered forlornly, anxiously awaiting the moment when he would start fucking me with his cock.

"That's correct, my little mate," he replied. "Do you feel as though you've been properly put in your place today?"

"Yes, sir," I whimpered, unsure of how much longer he

was going to make me wait. I felt as though I was ready to shatter into pieces and I sincerely hoped he'd let me.

"Good," he said and swiftly, he thrust in and out of me in rough motions. I gasped with pleasure, even as my body pinched hard in an effort to get used to his enormous size. It hurt but it also felt immeasurably good and I found that I wanted more, so much more.

His hands wound around my hips and he dug them into me, pressing me down against the boulder and holding me firmly in place. He took complete control of me as he fucked me, slowly at first before he started to pick up the momentum of his thrusts.

My core twisted hard at finally being given what I desperately wanted. He drove into me roughly, using me as hard as he desired. His pelvis slapped against my punished pussy and it felt like I was getting spanked there all over again. His cock speared into me, taking me and twisting me into a wet little mess that simply wanted to be used hard. It pressed into me deeply and I shuddered with desire.

My nipples hardened into tight little peaks, pushing against the hard surface of the rock beneath me. The pressure against my spanked breasts was painful but it only served to heighten my arousal to levels I hadn't thought myself capable of.

I was so hot. My body was smoldering with unreleased pleasure and I struggled to manage it. He fucked me even harder and I whined with need. I wanted to come badly. My inner walls shuddered around his length and I squeezed his cock, milking him for everything that he gave me.

"Please," I begged.

"You are not allowed to come yet, omega. You will wait for permission," he commanded, and a hot streak of desire arced straight down to my clit. I trembled as pleasure overwhelmed me and I knew it was only a matter of time before I lost control of it completely.

The longer he fucked me, the more I felt his dominance over me. He owned my pain, my pleasure, and my body and that became quite clear as he thrust into me as roughly as he pleased. I whimpered and writhed as he used me, suffering under the sheer weight of the passion that was raging inside me.

I begged him and pleaded for permission. He only used me harder and even more ruthlessly than before. He was enjoying this power over me and I could feel every last inch it as it slammed into my pussy again and again.

"Please, sir. I can't," I pleaded, no longer able to form complete sentences. I lost my words and struggled to piece them together, focused entirely on the pleasure humming through my veins and throbbing in between my thighs.

"Come hard for me, my little mate," he demanded, and I obeyed. I came for him. Hard.

A tremor raced through my body, a gentle warning of what was to come. I tried to fight it because I knew it would shatter me in a way that I'd never been shattered before. Heated bliss quaked inside me, intensifying with each passing moment until I was panting for air. I was so very hot. I needed to breathe, but most of all I needed release.

My entire body started to shake, and my muscles flexed. He'd built the perfect storm inside me and now it was breaking me apart as it all came to a head. At first, I moaned quietly with pleasure but before long, I was screaming with it.

He used me hard as I came, not caring that it hurt, but that made my orgasm all that much stronger. I trembled under its power as it swept me into its thrall. My blood felt like it was boiling beneath my skin and I felt myself tense as a second orgasm swept over me far too quickly after the first.

No man had ever made me come like this. He fucked me harder and I knew in that moment that he would be the last man I ever fucked.

He was my mate. I was his and his cock was teaching me that with every last thrust.

"That's it, mate. Come all over my cock," he purred, and my core clenched down hard. My pussy tightened around that large cock and I took it all. I took it all because that's what he demanded of me.

Decadent bliss hurtled through me and I found it as pleasurable as it was painful. I'd been so tightly wound up by his punishment that every orgasm felt like it fractured me into pieces and as a third one threatened to break over me, I keened loudly.

My legs shook and my toes and fingers curled as my ecstasy ravaged me from within. Endless bliss washed over me and it felt like it was going to break me apart. His hips slapped against my still very sore little pussy, punishing my scalded flesh with every last incredible thrust. He slammed into me again and again as I came for him.

I don't know how many orgasms he forced from my body. It didn't matter. I was going to keep coming until he decided to allow me to stop.

"I can't," I pleaded.

"You will," he answered.

He used me hard and rough, claiming my pussy and showing me that not only could he punish me with his palm and a switch, but that his cock was just as formidable too. My pussy ached from his enormous length, but that didn't stop him. In fact, it only made him piston into me with a ferocious vigor that spoke of his powerful otherworldly virility.

I came so many times that soon I began to fear each subsequent one.

I had thought my punishment had ended with that last fateful lash of the switch on my poor little clit. I soon realized I had been wrong.

He was punishing me hard with that enormous cock. An intoxicating mix of pleasure raced through my veins and I struggled to take it. I screamed. I moaned and I writhed from the intensity of the sensations coursing through my ravaged little body. As he fucked me, I started to fully understand what it meant to be subdued.

He lifted my hips off the rock and wound his arm around my waist, holding my lower body in midair, which made me take his cock even more deeply. He reached around my waist and toyed with my aching clit. Then he pinched it hard and I broke into pieces beneath him.

The next few orgasms hurt far more than the rest. He punished my sore, needy clit with his fingers, dragging out every ounce of pleasure from me that he could. I struggled to take each one, but it didn't matter. I came because he demanded it.

His fingers were ruthless as he fucked me. Each orgasm tore through me like a riptide. My fingers clawed at the boulder as I felt every bit the naughty punished little mate. I felt his dominance and most of all, I felt his complete control over me. I couldn't stop coming for him, even if I wanted to.

His massive cock throbbed inside me and I still struggled to take it, but I didn't have a choice. My thighs flexed and I started to scream once more.

"These next few orgasms are going to remind you that you are right to fear me, mate. They're also going to remind you that no matter what happens, you're mine and that your rightful place is by my side, little omega," he warned.

I wailed as I realized what he was saying. I didn't know how much more I was capable of giving him. My body was his to control and he would force more pleasure from me if he wanted to.

Yesterday, I had been a respected scientist, a leader in my own right.

Today, I was an omega that had to be put in her place by her alpha.

My body shuddered with desire and I wailed as I felt myself edge toward my next orgasm. I knew even before it hit me that it was going to be more brutal than any of my previous orgasms and maybe even more vicious than all of the others combined.

"I want to hear you scream," he demanded.

I panted with the intense volleys of pleasure and pain cascading through me. I tried to fight the oncoming onslaught of agonizing ecstasy, but it was useless. My body was answering to my alpha's call.

He pinched my clit hard and the first orgasm of many inevitably followed.

I lost control. In that moment, I became utterly and completely his.

I broke incredibly hard.

Ruthless pleasure devoured me from the inside out. The pain and pleasure came together in a savagely intoxicating mixture that cut me from within. I felt like I was falling into a black hole of cruel bliss and there wasn't any way for me to claw myself out. I writhed beneath him and my clit pulsed hard in between his punishing fingers. Then he twisted my poor little bud, ensuring that my orgasm was just as painful as it was pleasurable.

I screamed and before I knew what was happening, I came so hard that I started to sob.

Brutal ecstasy tore me into pieces, and I fractured on his cock. His fingers cut into my hip and then he spanked my pussy with his hand, and I came once more. I shattered and my pussy desperately clutched at his cock, even as he continued to use my tight channel as roughly as he pleased.

Tears streamed down my cheeks as he fucked me. He forced one orgasm after the next from my worn-out little body. I had no idea how many times I came. I just knew how much each one now hurt. I wept as he forced them from my body, one after another.

He'd used my need for him against me. He'd taught me what a true punishment was like. Sobs racked my frame and I tried to suck in one breath after another and still he used me hard. Soon, I was terrified that this fucking wouldn't ever end. He didn't even remotely show any signs of slowing down and that scared me.

I came again and my core twisted hard with pain as passion raged on inside me.

I sobbed even harder.

"You will come for me one last time, little omega, before your punishment is complete. This final orgasm will ensure that you are never left unsure of your place ever again. Do you understand me?"

"Yes, sir," I wailed.

He circled my clit with his fingers, building my need with each passing motion until I could feel that final orgasm edging closer. I feared that inevitable pleasure more than all the rest and I cried as I realized my unavoidable fate.

I was so very, very sore and I was going to orgasm. Again.

I was going to come for my alpha because that's what he had commanded of me.

"Come now, omega," he ordered.

I obeyed because I had no other choice.

I sobbed through every last second of that orgasm, even as pleasure blazed through me with an agonizing heat that was more intense than I had ever known. It eviscerated me from within, breaking over me with the power of an unstoppable tidal wave. I hurtled off the edge of a cliff into boundless painful bliss and drowned in it. I writhed and moaned, shamefully screaming with my release as I splayed my thighs, all while he fucked me roughly and as hard as he wanted to. His cock speared into my pussy, punishing my tight little hole even as my sore clit pulsed with my release.

When it was all over, I continued to cry, thoroughly mastered by my alpha. My body pulsed with sensation and every inch of me hurt. He pulled free of me and lifted me up off the boulder, only to deposit me in front of him on my knees.

His cock was impossibly erect right in front of my eyes. I gulped and looked up at him, remembering his warnings of what I was going to have to do with my tongue.

"Open your mouth. It's time that you show me that you learned your lesson," he said darkly, and my sore pussy pulsed with want.

I licked my lips, tasting the salt from my tears.

His palm caressed the side of my cheek and his fingers brushed what remained of my tears from my face. I sniffed and tried to pull myself together, fully feeling the weight of what he'd put me through. I whimpered softly and he continued to comfort me with that palm.

When I'd gathered as much of my composure as I could, I opened my lips and tentatively moved forward toward his cock.

"Would you like to make it up to me now, my sweet mate?" he asked gently.

"Yes, sir," I whispered, my voice hoarse from all the screaming.

"Good girl," he said, and he used his fingers to lift my chin a little higher before he pushed his cock in between my waiting lips.

Even though I was thoroughly exhausted, I wanted to

please. I wanted to show him that I was sorry for what I had done and that I now understood what would happen when a naughty little mate who disobeyed her alpha.

I wrapped my lips around his thick length. My movements were hesitant at first, but the more I suckled him, the bolder I grew. I could taste the musky sweetness of my own arousal. The taste of myself was all over his cock and I lapped at him with my tongue. Carefully, I lifted his length with my fingers and softly kissed the spot I had tased. It was still pink, and I cautiously licked at it with the tip of my tongue, trying to soothe it as much as I could. He groaned and I doubled my efforts to bathe him with my tongue before I returned my mouth to the head of his cock.

"I've marked your beautiful bare bottom and your perfect breasts. I've welted your wet little pussy, but there's one last place I want to mark today before your punishment ends, sweet omega," he purred as he rolled his hips, pressing his cock deeper into my mouth. I didn't respond.

"I'm going to mark that pretty throat. You're going to be a good little girl, aren't you? You're going to swallow everything I give you," he continued, and my pussy clenched tightly in anticipation. I worshipped him with my mouth, taking care to clean off all the evidence of my own arousal from his cock. The taste of him washed over my tongue, one of pure masculinity and salty virility. I found that I couldn't get enough of it.

His fingers dug into my hair and fisted at the base of my scalp as he took control of my tentative explorations.

"Such a good girl," he purred and then his hips pumped forward as he claimed my mouth as his too.

His movements were harsh at first and I struggled to draw in air as he fucked my throat. Before long I learned to suck in each breath as he pulled out of me. I did my best to suckle him, using my tongue to circle around his length as much as possible even when he was using me so roughly.

Soon enough, my throat was just as sore as the rest of me and I struggled not to let even more tears fall as he used me. After everything my punishment had entailed, this made me feel more out of control than anything else. He fucked my throat hard and just when I thought I was going to begin to cry again, his cock throbbed against my tongue.

My pussy tightened with want. He was going to come in my throat, and I had to swallow every last drop. With shame, I realized I wanted exactly that. I needed it and he was going to give it to me.

His thrust became more erratic, less controlled and I knew he was close. I opened for him and felt the first pulse of his seed spurt against the back of my throat. I swallowed around him, using everything in me to take each heated burst of cum down into my belly. I moaned around him as he came in my mouth, feeling his member throb on my tongue. I worshipped his cock with my lips and my tongue until the very last drops of his seed slipped down my throat.

He groaned with utter satisfaction.

I'd pleased him and that thrilled me far more than I expected it to.

He pulled free from my lips and bent down to lift me to my feet. Carefully, he sat down on the boulder and situated me in his lap so that my head lay against his shoulder.

He held me.

"I'm very proud of you, little omega. You took your punishment very well. It's all over now," he murmured, and I curled into him, desperate to feel his arms around me. He'd taken me and broken me into pieces, and right now, I knew he was the only one who could put me together again.

I found myself crying silently as he held me, and I was surprised by it. I hid my face in his shoulder and his fingers gently stroked through my hair. It was soothing and my tears soon dried as I gathered myself and tried to piece myself back together again. I whimpered softly and those same fingers drifted up and down my back. My breathing slowly returned to normal and I pressed my forehead against his chest, allowing the scent of him to give me comfort.

"Such a good little mate," he murmured, and my heart leapt into my throat. I wasn't sure why those simple words made me feel so whole, but they did. His strong arms surrounded me, a secure and safe place that promised never to let go. His fingertips brushed the strands of hair that were stuck to my forehead aside and then he lifted my chin to look into my eyes.

"Such a beautiful little thing," he murmured, and I couldn't help but smile a bit in return. He ran his thumb along my cheekbone and electric tingles rushed straight down to my core even after all he'd put me through. He did it again and I shivered at its strange magical effect.

I shouldn't be falling for him. He'd stripped, spanked, and switched me. He'd fucked me too. I should be furious. I should fight back, but even as my mind fought the connection, I could feel myself wanting to know more. Even now with my ear pressed against his chest, I could hear the beat of his heart and knew it was in tune with mine.

"Kiba," I whispered.

"What is it, little mate?"

"This. What I feel. Is it always like this?" I asked.

"We are fated mates, sweet girl. I am the alpha and you are my omega. The two of us were destined to be together. We were meant to find each other. You are mine and you will bear my children. The two of us will continue the shifter line, ensuring that the pack continues on for the next several hundred years until the next alpha arises," he explained.

"Your children," I repeated softly.

"Yes. Our beta offspring will be fertile for several generations, ensuring that the pack remains viable for a good long while," he explained.

I'd never thought about being a mother. It had never been a part of my vision for the future, at least not until now. For some reason, thinking about having children with Kiba seemed right and the more I thought about it, the more I realized that I wanted it too.

I shouldn't be feeling these things. It was too soon, too fast. But the longer he held me in his arms and the more I breathed in his perfect scent, the more connected to him I felt and the more I never wanted to leave his side.

Maybe it was magic or maybe it was truly fate, but either way, I was his now. The residual ache across my breasts and my backside, as well as inside my throat and my pussy, was a constant reminder of that, as was the continual beat of my heart.

"That hurt," I whined.

"It was supposed to," he chuckled softly. I pouted and he lightly patted my cheek with his hand. "You needed a very thorough lesson because you were disobedient. As a result, I had to punish you in order to teach you your rightful place."

My pussy clenched tightly at his words. I couldn't bear to meet his eyes, so I turned away, feeling myself blush at my body's traitorous reaction. His fingers returned to my chin and he forced me to meet his gaze once more. I fidgeted and hummed with shame, even as his fingers drifted across my thigh. I squirmed as those same fingers pressed between my legs and into my moist folds. I was wet for him once more.

"You were made for me, little mate. I am pleased to find you this way for me, even after I've already made you come for me many times today. Your body knows its master," he said quietly, and the rumble of his seductive voice made my legs tremble a little with need.

For a while, the two of us were silent. I stayed in his lap and he held me gently the entire time. I enjoyed his embrace and the quiet as I tried to come to terms with all that had happened to me in the last forty-eight hours.

"They're going to be looking for me back there. The government paid a lot of money to bring me in to study your kind," I finally said, and he grunted in acknowledgement. I pushed against his chest and sat up straight, staring at him more boldly now.

"They'll come after me," I added.

"I imagine they will," he replied.

"That does not worry you?" I asked and he shook his head.

"It doesn't because we're going to be long gone by the time they start looking," he answered.

"You're not going to bring me back?" I questioned him.

"No. I'm not," he said curtly. I chewed at my lip, trying to process this information.

"They brought me in to complete a job," I answered.

"You have a new one and that is to be by my side, mate," he replied as he stared into my eyes, his gaze dangerous. "You will do well to remember that."

I pressed my lips together. I was never one to sit back and just let others dictate how I lived my life, but now was not the time to push him, not after the punishment I'd just been given by his hand.

"Where will you take me?" I decided to ask instead.

"South. There is another facility holding my betas prisoner. We will go there and free them."

"How do you know?"

"I can sense them, just like I could with you, little omega," he replied.

I shivered against him.

"Come, it's time to meet up with the others," he dictated.

"I have no clothes," I said with a pout.

"You won't need them. You will remain naked until I decide that you've earned the privilege of clothing once again," he commanded.

My nipples peaked and my pussy clamped down hard. I didn't know why I'd reacted that way, but I couldn't deny that I liked it.

CHAPTER 6

Kiba

My mate was perfect. Mine. I loved the way her body responded to me even as her mind fought her rightful place. The connection between us went far deeper than she was aware of though. I had felt it the moment I'd laid my eyes on her. It was the omega within her. It answered only to me as the alpha, *her* alpha. It was written deep into her genetic code, only released and activated once I arose from the earth. It was as though a tether tied our hearts together as one, a magical link between us demanding that I breed her as hard and fast as possible.

I was a patient man though. She would be bred in due time, but it had to be when she was safe and sound. I would not have her pregnant and in danger as we traveled and fought to release the betas that the government was still holding captive. I gritted my teeth together, allowing the smoldering anger inside me to brew to life. They were my people. They did not deserve to be held prisoner and I would do everything in my power to ensure their freedom, no matter what it took.

I did not know much about this government my mate spoke of, but I would question her about it. I could ask one of my betas, but I would rather she speak to me and tell me of her world. I would listen and she would tell me. I wanted to know more about her. I wanted to know everything there was to know. I craved the sound of her voice.

The moment I'd laid my eyes on her, I'd known that she would be mine forever. Her brilliant green eyes were flecked with shades of blue and chocolate brown, colors of Mother Nature and of the earth itself. Her golden blonde hair was long and free and hung down to the middle of her back. The gentle breeze made it sway in the wind, swirling around her toned body in a way that was both alluring and awe-inspiring.

I wanted to take her into my arms and make love to her once more. She was a flawless picture of beauty and perfection. My mate.

I didn't do any either of those things though. Instead, I took her hand and gently helped her to her feet. I took a few seconds to admire her naked form and the way her pert breasts swung a little with her movements, both large enough to fill the palms of my hands. Her lean stomach gave way to curvy hips. Toned thighs spoke to the care she took in her body, a silent measure of the strength within her.

Her feet remained protected in her shoes and I would see that they stayed that way. I was used to walking barefoot but her skin was delicate and soft, easily broken by a sharp rock or jagged branch. Lifting up her hand, I walked around her and assessed the marks I'd left behind on her skin. Her bottom was crisscrossed with little welts all across her skin and was still quite pink from my palm. Her breasts were marked less so, as I'd take a lighter hand to them. Her pussy had tiny little lines that spoke to the very thorough switching she'd received there too.

She'd remain welted for the rest of the day. They would disappear overnight. She'd been punished and would be quite sore, but I'd never really mar her perfect dewy skin.

Her fingers tightened around mine and I lifted my gaze to see a rosy blush highlight her cheekbones. I liked that I had that effect on her. I'd have to admire her naked body like this more often.

"Come. Let's meet up with the rest of the pack," I suggested, and she nodded slightly. There was a sparkle in her eye, and I studied her more closely, sensing a streak of rebelliousness within her still, even after a spanking, switching, and a great many forced orgasms.

Should she defy me, I had many more ways to break her. I had a feeling she'd learn about them one day, maybe even one day soon.

* * *

DURING THE WALK to where I'd instructed the pack to gather, I questioned Dawn about the inner workings of her government. She answered what she could and described how it all worked to the best of her ability. I learned the Department of Paranormal Activity had jumped into her life only just yesterday, taking her and depositing her in a world where shifters like me were real. It baffled me that she hadn't known of our kind or the other types of paranormal creatures that walked the land with us, but I didn't voice my surprise.

She hadn't known about me or her role as an omega. She'd known none of that. Now though, I was going to teach her about all of it. I was going to bring her into my world.

I held her hand loosely and she held mine. Her fingers were soft and small, fitting perfectly in mine because they were made for it.

When I noticed that the sun was starting to descend in the sky, I shifted into my wolf form and instructed Dawn to climb onto my back. I knelt down for her and her small fingers grasped at my fur as she pulled herself up onto my shoulders.

"Hold on. Wrap your arms around my throat. I'm going to run, and I want you secure," I told her. I felt her thighs press against me and then her arms wound around me. Her hold was tight. She was strong and I was even more sure of it now.

I took off into the woods. My gait was slow at first as she balanced herself on my spine, learning to move with my body as I ran. Gradually though, her grip grew tighter and surer as I traveled, and I began to increase my pace until I was sprinting at full speed.

Running like this felt like freedom and it was at times like these that I felt most connected with the magic of the earth. The wind caressed through the strands of my fur and I ran even harder. My muscles warmed at the exertion and it made me feel alive, knowing my pack was waiting for my return. They were going to meet my mate for the first time, and I couldn't wait to show her off.

The hours passed and the sun set, giving way to twinkling stars overhead. The crescent moon rose on the horizon, and its light cut down to the forest floor. My eyes were well adjusted to the darkness of the wilds though. I was made for traveling like this, either in the full light of day or in the shadows of night.

My claws dug into the dirt beneath my feet, propelling me forward with every step. Dawn's breathing was quick, showcasing her excitement and exhilaration as she hugged her arms around my neck. I could feel her joy and that impelled me to move even faster. I crossed one mile after the next and before long, I could feel that my pack was close. I called for them and told them to prepare for my arrival.

Before long, I could smell the aroma of venison cooking on an open campfire. The place I'd chosen for my pack was inaccessible from the ground for most humans. The forest was dense, and their planes couldn't land between the trees or the mountains. Much of the trails into the area were overgrown and not well traveled. My wolves had gone deep and as I made my way to them, I was even more sure that this was a good place to shelter and regroup as the once-captive members took their rightful places in my pack.

"We're ready for your arrival, alpha," one of my female betas answered.

"Good," I answered. *"I have retrieved my mate. You all will give your respect to the omega upon my return."*

Every single beta there would have heard me. They would know that I was coming and that I had found my mate, that I was carrying with me the future of the pack.

Not long after, I broke out into a small clearing where my pack was waiting. There was a least a hundred of them now, spread out amongst the grass and in the trees. They were all in wolf form and it was a sight to behold as every single one of them bowed their heads in reverence to me and my mate. I stopped, knelt down and allowed Dawn to climb off my back. She blushed again beautifully, and I smiled knowingly. It shamed her to be naked in front of the pack, but her nipples peaked, and I knew that pretty pussy would be soaked when I inspected it later.

She'd get used to it sooner or later.

I nodded in greeting and Dawn stepped tentatively to my side, looking around in awe at what she saw. It was likely that she'd never seen so many wolves in her life, let alone beasts like this. She wasn't scared though, and I was proud of her for it. Her fingers dug gently into my shoulder and then she leaned against me for support.

I glanced into the clearing and noticed the brightly burning campfire. I sniffed the air and chuckled when I heard Dawn's stomach growl with hunger. I moved a step away and shifted back to my human form.

"This is Dawn, my mate and the omega. You will show her respect, or you will answer to me." I waited and the wolves all around us began to howl in unison. The effect of their combined voices was powerful.

"We welcome her as one of our own," they answered as one.

"Thank you," she murmured softly, her delicate voice wavering with wonder. I smiled and nodded my approval, before taking her hand in mine once more.

"Come now, let's eat and you can meet the members of my pack," I said loudly and all around me the betas began to shift. At once, the clearing was filled with humans rather than wolves. Voices rumbled all around us and I saw Dawn visibly relax.

"It's not so bad being naked when everyone else is naked too," she whispered in my ear. I openly laughed before I smacked her bottom. She yelped softly in surprise more than anything else.

"Perhaps, but you're the only one here with a pink welted bottom, aren't you," I countered, and her blush deepened.

"Yes, alpha," she answered timidly, her voice dropping several decibels as I stood over her. Her dismay amused me, and I grinned back at her.

"Don't worry. I'm sure you'll see many a spanked bottom the more time that you spend with the pack. There is a distinct hierarchy among the betas and oftentimes, many an errant female needs to be reminded of her place over her mate's thighs. Just like I imagine you will need to be. Perhaps if you earn it, I'll even take you in hand with everyone watching."

She blushed even harder. I really enjoyed that.

"You wouldn't," she exclaimed. I simply grinned in return and watched her squirm under my scrutiny. I leaned back and imagined her shame and arousal the moment I forced her over my knees for a spanking. I fantasized about the wetness I'd find between her thighs as a result. I wondered how hard she would come for me if I fucked her in front of the pack in order to fully remind her that her place was right beneath me.

I growled with my desire for her tight little body and she pressed her thighs together in response. I sniffed the air and growled again. A soft moan escaped her lips at my sounds and her eyes fluttered closed. Her head dipped, her shoulders rounded forward, and I watched as she shuddered hard for me.

I'd had her only hours ago and I wanted her again. She needed to eat though. I hadn't forgotten that. With her escape from the facility early this morning, she had not eaten anything at all.

Once she had though, all bets were off. I would take her, and I'd take her hard. Over and over until she screamed for me to stop.

I guided her over to a boulder near the fire. One of the female betas offered her a blanket, and she gratefully took it. My kind ran several degrees hotter than humans and Dawn was only human here.

"Thank you, Rebecca. It's good to see that you made it out of there safely," Dawn said, and I cocked my head as I stared at her.

"You know her?" I asked.

"I met her yesterday. She was one of the captive betas and showed me her wolf form at my request," she answered.

Rebecca sat down on the ground beside the campfire on a spot of grass. Deferentially, she turned her head toward me.

"I told her that you were coming for us. I sensed she was your mate, alpha, so I thought I would give her insight into what was coming. She'd come to study us and understand why the betas were restless when the real reason was that you had arrived," Rebecca explained.

"Thank you, Rebecca," I replied, and she smiled softly. There had been a slight edge of nervousness in her eyes when she had begun to speak, and I was pleased to see it disappear as I acknowledged her.

"Did all the betas held captive with you make it out?" Dawn questioned quietly.

Rebecca's eyes turned to mine for permission and I nodded.

"They did. The pack left no one behind," she answered.

"And Dr. Livingston?" Dawn asked next.

"I never saw him, nor did I catch his scent. He probably stayed hidden in his rooms until the all clear alarm sounded," Rebecca explained, and Dawn sighed in relief.

"This man is important to you?" I questioned.

"He was my mentor, a teacher to me. I was hoping he didn't get hurt," she replied.

"My people didn't go in with the intention to kill or hurt anyone. Their mission was to break their kindred free and only fight as necessary. The aim was to sneak as far inside as we could without alerting the humans," I said further. "We do not want war, only to free our people."

She nodded, processing my words as the moments passed by. When she was finished, she turned back toward me and Rebecca tended to the skewers of meat cooking over the fire.

"So, what's next?" she asked.

"We free the rest of my betas and you're going to help us do it."

CHAPTER 7

Dawn

I HADN'T EXPECTED any of this. Yesterday I'd been just a scientist researching how stem cells worked and today I was completely bare in a massive group of naked wolf shifters. I swallowed in disbelief as I considered my foreseeable future. Was this my life now?

It was nice to have a familiar face here with me in Rebecca. As Kiba spoke, she'd brushed her fingers along my shoulder in kinship and I'd smiled at her kindness. She understood how very difficult this was for me because she'd met me before Kiba had taken me as his mate. She'd been the one to warn me he was coming, and she'd been the reason I'd known exactly who he was the moment that I'd set eyes on him.

Sitting next to the fire with her, I appraised her, and she smiled in my direction. I had a feeling that she and I would be good friends. She handed me a skewer of grilled venison and I took it. I was starving and I blushed thinking about the fact that I'd worked up quite the appetite in the woods earlier this morning.

A group of betas gathered around the fire and watched as Kiba took the largest skewer. After he began to eat, the others followed in kind, sharing skewers of meat between them. I blew on the warm venison and when it was cool enough, plucked a piece off with my fingers and popped it into my mouth. It tasted incredibly fresh and juicy. It was so good that I polished off the entire skewer of meat before I smacked my lips together with pleasure.

"Compliments to the chef," I exclaimed and the betas nearest to me laughed.

"Glad you liked it," Rebecca said with a wink. "It's not a burger though. What I wouldn't give for one from that little diner on Main Street in Helena." Her eyes had a sad sort of look to them. It was as if she was somewhere else entirely.

"When was the last time you were free?" I asked her.

"It's been at least fifty years. It's a gift to finally feel the sun and the light of the moon on my face again instead of that awful fluorescent lighting they used in our cells," she replied.

"You were prisoner for that long?"

She simply nodded. I knew how old she was, that betas were essentially ageless as soon as they reached a certain age. Still, that was a really long time to remain in that small cell. I couldn't imagine being kept from the sun like that. When work overwhelmed me and the stress from another deadline felt like too much, I'd go for a walk alone and gather my thoughts. The concept of having that taken away for so very long was both saddening and horrifying at the same time. My trepidation over these strange new people faded as the night when on, when I saw the brilliant smiles on the faces of those that I'd seen held prisoner only yesterday. I began to see them all very differently for what each one of them had gone through.

Sure, I might feel sad that I no longer have my science to fill my day, but at least I was free. These betas didn't always have that. Now they did. They'd earned their freedom and there were more like them out there, unfairly held captive because the government thought they were dangerous, the ultimate predator. Maybe they were. Maybe they weren't, but either way, they didn't deserve to remain behind bars when they were innocent of any wrongdoing.

Some of the betas were singing and others were dancing. A big male beta was throwing more wood on the fire and another was whittling something with a knife.

It was peaceful. An innocent demonstration of the enjoyment of life.

I pulled my shoulders back and met Kiba's eyes. In that moment, I decided that my career was no longer important. As much as I wanted to fight my fate as his mate, the members of his pack were my people now. Hopefully one day, I'd consider them family.

I was going to fight for what was right. I was going to fight for their freedom.

"I will help you free the rest of the betas," I said softly, and he smiled softly and beckoned me over to him. I went willingly and he held out a hand before he helped me to climb back into his lap. I felt so small when I sat with him like this. I breathed in his scent once more and my heart fluttered with desire.

Was this happiness? Was Kiba my destiny?

"Rebecca over there was a teacher. She taught science and math before she was taken as she was leaving her job in Helena late one night. She'd been alone and lived mostly in solitude. She's never hurt anyone, and they held her captive for fifty years because of it," he explained softly, and I pressed my face into his shoulder.

"It isn't right," I whispered.

"I know, sweet mate. Her story isn't unique either. Some of the prisoners held with her were there for even longer, some shorter. None of them had done anything wrong but your government held them captive because of the potential danger they could bring to the world," he answered.

"Because your kind is stronger than us," I added.

"Perhaps," Kiba answered.

"I've seen the betas fight. I've seen their fur deflect the bullets. The security guards were unprepared. They didn't even have knives," I said.

"In our wolf forms, we are nearly immortal. Bullets are unable to penetrate through our thick fur and skin. Knives will hardly leave a scratch. In our human forms, we are weak to both weapons and that has been the downfall of many betas over the years. We can die from a fall or a car crash or an unforeseeable accident just as humans can. But we do have one particular weakness that's as deadly to our wolf forms as it is to our human ones," he continued.

I watched the fire pop and listened to its crackle, remembering what the wolves looked like in battle. I'd seen the very things Kiba had talked about that morning. I'd seen how invincible the wolves had been and how the humans had the distinct disadvantage in almost every way. I'd seen the humans' inevitable loss.

I lifted my head and stared into his eyes.

"What is it?"

"Silver," he answered.

"Really? Like in the movies?" I chewed my lip.

"Yes. Although we're distant relatives to the werewolf, we retain the same weakness. We've kept it a closely guarded secret though and it seems that your Department of Paranormal Activity assumed it was just a myth as they didn't attack any of my people with silver bullets or blades. We may not always be so lucky, but we have to take our wins as they come," he continued.

"I wouldn't have ever guessed," I murmured. He traced his fingers along my shoulder and up into my hair, petting me softly until I hummed in pleasure.

"It's my role to lead them but I also must keep them safe. As my mate, I trust that you will share that with me because now they are your people too. You're a part of the pack and that means you are family now. They will protect you as we protect them," he whispered, and each word seemed to sink down into my soul. I felt connected to them.

I knew then that what he said was true. I'd always been a loner, always stuck with my head in a book or in an office or holed up in lab late into the hours of the night. I didn't have to be that way any longer. These people were my pack now.

I watched as they sang and danced together, as they smiled and joked together. Couples were kissing and friends were laughing.

There was one thing missing though.

Children. Not a single one ran around, giggling and toasting marshmallows over the fire or sword fighting with sticks or doing cartwheels in the grass.

The betas were infertile.

Not a single one of them could bear children, but now the alpha had arrived and taken me as his mate. My children would be able to breed, allowing the rest to have children once more so that the shifters could remain a part of this world.

Kiba and I brought the pack hope. I understood that now.

I curled into Kiba's arms, welcoming the peace he offered. Tomorrow I would think about the betas that were wrongly imprisoned and we'd all figure a way to free the rest of them. Tonight though, I would enjoy the arms of my alpha.

"Would you kiss me?" I ventured, my voice so quiet I was sure he wouldn't hear me.

He boldly took my chin in his fingers and caressed my lower lip with his thumb before he pulled me into a kiss that was so gentle and soft that it left me breathless. It was tender but so thorough that my heart felt like it was going to beat out of my chest. My breath became his and, in that moment, we were one. When his lips left mine, I drew in a gulp of air and lifted my eyes to meet his.

I was naked in his arms. He'd taken my world and turned it upside down in a matter of hours, but now as I stared into those liquid blue irises, I saw something else. I saw my future, together with him. My skin tingled, a feeling unlike I'd ever experienced before. It was magical, an enchanted pull between us that I could no longer deny. It was like the earth beneath our feet was pushing us together to be one.

He was the alpha. I was the omega.

We were fated to be together. I was his and he was mine.

It felt as if the very air itself was calling for our union.

Maybe it was.

His arms tightened around me and I wondered if he could feel it too.

* * *

When the sun rose the next day, the pack seemed restless and anxious. Kiba quickly took control and started gathering the betas and instructing them on what the next few days would bring. He sent some ahead to hunt, while the rest he directed to follow the two of us.

We were beginning our journey to rescue the betas that morning. It was going to be a long and hard trek through the woods, but everyone's faces remained serious and an ominous feeling came over the pack as we prepared for the journey.

Kiba and I didn't get any time alone together that day. Occasionally though, I would feel his fingers caress my back and a sliver of happiness would hurtle through me. I knew he was thinking of me and despite the soreness in my body from his hard use of me the day before, I couldn't wait for the opportunity for it to happen once again.

When it was time to leave, the entire pack shifted into wolf form. Kiba knelt down and I climbed up onto his back, holding onto his strong neck as he took those first fateful steps toward freeing the rest of his betas.

I traveled with all of them for the next several days. Kiba led them south, through the mountains and the deep forests, taking care to keep to less traveled routes during the night. The stars and the rising moon guided the pack and the more time that I spent with them, the more I began to love them, and see that they were real people with feelings and hopes and dreams.

Toward the end of the journey, I could feel Kiba begin to tense along with the rest of the pack. When I asked what the cause was, he told me that we were drawing close to the second beta containment facility. I couldn't feel them, but he could. I didn't say a word as he chose a place where the pack could safely camp out for the rest of the day.

He found a hidden cave and as everyone began to settle, Kiba chose three of the fastest members of the pack to scout ahead. They ran off and Kiba assigned a rotation of guards to ensure the camp remained undisturbed. I curled up against his dark fur and his tail wrapped around me, keeping me snug and warm against his massive body. I slept, exhausted from the days of travel and lack of rest. I dreamed of what might come next when we set out to rescue the betas still kept prisoner.

The scouts returned that night and Kiba pulled them aside along with me. He introduced them to me as Flint, Ashe, and Nikita. They were slender, strong, and three of the younger members of the pack. They remained in wolf form, as did Kiba. It was safer for them that way.

"What do you have to report?" Kiba asked calmly, sitting back on his haunches and appraising the three wolves.

"We have much to tell you. This complex is much more heavily guarded than the first. It's even more remote and reachable only via a few gated access roads. The woods are less dense there and the terrain rockier, but with plenty of brush to cover our wolf forms," Flint began.

"There's a tall barbed wire fence surrounding the compound. The building itself appears to descend an unknown number of levels below ground as the first government black site did. It's patrolled by guards twenty-four/seven. There are cameras that are trained on the perimeter that appear to be running twenty-four/seven," Nikita reported.

"Our strategy is going to have to be different for this rescue mission," Kiba replied carefully.

"We saw a delivery truck arrive while we were there," Ashe offered, her feminine voice soft but confident.

"Before you rose, alpha, I worked for a site like this one," Nikita offered. *"There are a number of us with inside knowledge as to how their security systems work. We can devise a way to break into the compound, but we must become familiar with every detail of this particular black site's operations first. We need to do some reconnaissance."*

"Gather a small team. You will observe the facility and report every last detail. Once we have the information we need, we will devise a relevant strategy that will free our people for good," Kiba

directed and the three wolves dispersed as though they were shadows in the night.

Kiba shifted next to me and the magical feeling of his transformation tingled across my skin. When I turned my head, he was standing there beside me, human once more.

"When it comes time to free our beta kindred, you will remain here. It won't be safe for you. As strong as you are, your human body is still delicate and weak to the weaponry we may encounter there," he said softly. "Do you understand, little mate?"

"I do," I answered, but I didn't agree. I didn't voice my opinion, but my knowledge and expertise could prove useful if necessary. Not only that, but these wolves were quickly becoming a family to me. As a member of the pack, it was my right to be there for them too. I kept quiet though, knowing now was not the time to bring up how I felt.

Sometimes it was just easier to ask for forgiveness afterwards instead of asking for permission first.

We didn't talk of it again and before I knew it, a week had passed, and Nikita's team had completed their reconnaissance mission. They had taken detailed records of every single guard change during the day as well as when and where the delivery trucks arrived. Their notes included how the extensive gate operating system worked. Her team had also found an abandoned factory building nearby, which included some older computer equipment as well as some other leftover supplies from the black site compound.

Now that we had the information we needed, it was time to come up with a plan. Kiba and the pack were ready. It was time to free the rest of the betas.

* * *

AFTER FINDING no evidence of surveillance or human presence at the abandoned warehouse, we moved into it and used it as our base of operations. Kiba put Nikita in charge and she started planning and putting everything into motion.

In the next few days, I learned a great deal about the pack, but the most surprising thing of all was how skilled they were. They'd lived long lives and as a result, they'd worked a great many different careers, including quite a few in the technology sector. A number of them had taken to careers deep underground, where they traded in things like money, power, and prestige through highly developed coding skills that allowed them to hack through whatever digital walls that were required, including the one that we were going to break into in just a few days.

Ashe was able to procure a copy of the black site's blueprints, including every door and keycard scan lock through some of her own connections on the dark web. Everyone took their time to study it, including me.

Nikita broke into the camera feeds, making sure to record several hours of footage to use that would cover our tracks during the day of the break-in. She marked the location of several rooms where there was storage for a number of things including weapons, combat gear, and guard uniforms in case any of us would need them.

Flint hacked into the delivery manifests of what was being shipped in and out of the black site facility. He also found the information for the schedules for the next two weeks of delivery, including the exact times in which the trucks would arrive and depart.

The plan was beginning to take shape.

Loosely, a team would intercept the next delivery, taking the place of the drivers and filling the truck with pack members instead of product. Then, when the truck was inside and secure within the facility, the team would break out and take over the receiving area as quietly as possible. Once they were in position, they would open the gates, which apparently could only be done from the inside since they were on their own private servers not connected to the outside network. It would be tough to make it through the building undetected, but Nikita thought we could slip in and out without being discovered.

The night before the break-in was to take place, most of the pack was resting in preparation for the big day ahead. Nikita wasn't though and Kiba had gone off to hunt with a number of the men in order to blow off some steam, leaving me alone for the night. I wandered to Nikita's side where she was studying the blueprints, making sure she knew the plan inside and out because she was going to be the one leading everyone into the fray.

"Nikita, you should get some rest too," I whispered, trying to keep my voice down so that I didn't wake the others.

"I have to be prepared," she countered quietly. She was worried. The rest of the pack had been too. Before they'd gone to sleep, they'd been quiet. Tense. There hadn't been any laughter that night. Everyone was nervous and I understood why.

"You are, Nikita. You're more than prepared, more than any of us. That's why Kiba put you in charge," I replied.

She turned her gaze toward me, those yellow flecked eyes assessing me in silence.

"Let me help you," I offered.

"I can't put you at risk, omega," she countered carefully. Her eyes narrowed at me in suspicion as she tried to read my expression.

"Ashe has been looking into the records that the black site kept, including the scientific information they stored on their server. She'd ignored those but when I asked to see them, she'd prepared the files for me. I looked through them.

This site was researching something different than I had been. Do you know what that was?" I asked carefully, keeping my gaze trained on her.

"No. I don't," she replied apprehensively.

"They knew all about shifters here. They didn't know of the existence of the alpha or anything like that, nor did they seem to care. No. They were researching two different things. One is the answer to why all of you are infertile after several generations. Two, how your kind lives for so very long. They were using you to answer two critical questions that humans have sought for a very long time, the key to infertility and more important, the answer to human immortality," I continued.

"Did they find what they were looking for?" she asked.

"Yes. And that's the reason why I need to join your team tomorrow. I need to break into the government lab to steal their samples. If I could take the formulas that they've generated for myself, it would ensure that the pack never has to want for anything again. We'd have the money to purchase our very own country, our own land where we could raise our children in the safety of the alpha."

She stared at me in silence. She knew what I was saying was true.

"You'd be safe. You might even be able to have your own children again," I said.

"My daughter died a long time ago," she answered.

"I'm sorry," I whispered. I reached for her, placing my fingers on her arm. She stilled under my touch, sighing with her sadness. She looked away for a moment and I could tell she was far away in her thoughts.

"The black death took her from me long ago, a disease that we can cure with a simple round of antibiotics today. She died in my arms, screaming for me to make it better and I couldn't. I didn't have any other children after that. I couldn't bear it," she said, gazing back into my eyes once more.

"Would you ever want to?"

"It took me a very long time to heal from her loss," she answered. She swallowed and turned away, crossing her arms over her chest.

"Let me join you. I can sneak into the lab and take what I need," I insisted.

She licked her lips and turned back to face me. Quickly, she grabbed my wrist and dragged me into the other room where we were alone, where she wouldn't be heard.

"There's a few abandoned guard uniforms in the storage closet. I'm not telling you to do this and I will vehemently deny any suggestion of it, but if you were to take one and sneak inside tomorrow, it would likely go unnoticed by the humans," she replied. "If Kiba ever finds out…"

"He won't. I will make sure of that," I answered, cutting her off before she said anything else.

She stared at me for a long moment, likely deciding if she should trust me or not.

"I'm acting on my own. You just mentioned the guard uniforms in passing and I decided to steal one for myself," I pressed and finally she nodded.

"I'm going to go to bed. I'm not going to come back till morning," she replied, her voice a little louder this time, loud enough for someone else to hear.

"Goodnight, Nikita," I responded.

She left the room and I was there all alone.

In silence, I prepared myself for my own mission that night. No one interrupted me as I studied the blueprints. I hid a uniform where no one else would look and I readied for the moment when I would break into the black site alongside with my pack. I palmed one of the knock-off master keycards Ashe had created and stored it in the pocket of the outfit I was going to wear tomorrow.

I was going to do what I had to do in order to make sure that my pack had the future it deserved and that my children would be safe and cared for no matter what. When Kiba finally put children in my belly, I wanted to be sure that their freedom would remain unhindered. I wanted to make sure they would survive.

When the sun finally rose, I felt ready. The pack was just beginning to get up too.

I watched as Nikita gathered her chosen members of her team. Ashe prepped her own group on the computer terminals we'd hacked into for our own gain. Flint outfitted the team with supplies, including keycards that he'd programmed himself on very loose lanyards around their necks. When in their wolf forms, it would fit them like a collar and would work to open any doors that had been programmed into its code.

My eyes flicked to the bushes outside the abandoned building, where I'd stashed my own keycard and uniform.

I felt Kiba at my side and I smiled, acting as if everything was normal. His fingers grazed against my shoulder and I realized I hardly even thought about being naked anymore. His chiseled bare chest pressed against my back and I bit my lip as his hard cock nestled against my bottom. My pussy tightened and I imagined what it would feel like for him to bend me over and fuck me here, right in front of the entire pack.

I blushed when I realized where my thoughts had gone. I took a deep breath and shoved them away, knowing I had to focus on my own mission ahead.

"When I return with the rest of my betas, I'm going to take you into the woods and fuck that little pussy hard enough to remind you that no matter what, I'm always going to be your alpha. When I'm finally through with you, that pretty pussy is going to be very sore because that's exactly how I want it," he whispered in my ear and I couldn't help myself as a moan escaped my lips despite everything in me trying to stop it.

My pussy tightened and his fingers caressed my hardened nipples.

"I can smell just how wet that makes you, my little mate," he murmured, and my hips unconsciously twitched in the direction of his cock.

"You will think of me when I'm gone. You may tease that little clit of yours from time to time, but you are not allowed to come. When I return, you'll be allowed to come all over my cock and not a moment before," he instructed, and I whimpered with need.

"Behave, little mate," he warned.

"I will, alpha," I answered.

"Good girl," he replied.

"Stay safe, Kiba," I finally managed to whisper.

He turned me around and leaned down, capturing me in a kiss that left me breathless and wanting. When he eventually pulled away from me, he stared down at me and I carefully schooled my expression, taking care to think only about the wetness between my thighs and not about the fact that I was going to deliberately break into the black site compound despite his explicit instructions that I not get involved. His eyes narrowed a little in suspicion and I rounded my shoulders, reaching for him and capturing his fingers in mine. I squeezed them gently and the look of apprehension he was giving me softened.

Nikita called for him and I released his hand. He turned and I knew he was going to focus on the pack for the day, rather than me. I slipped into the woods and waited for the pack to begin to move. It wouldn't be long now.

Kiba and his group took off first, assigned the task of taking over the delivery truck while it was in route to the black site compound. His team would ensure that Nikita's much smaller one could hide inside the back of the truck and break the betas out from within while also allowing the rest of the pack into the complex.

It would turn into organized chaos, which would prove perfect for my own mission.

When the abandoned building area was deserted of all members of the pack, I made my way out of the woods and retrieved my supplies. I pulled on the guard uniform, grateful for the shield mask designed to protect my face from danger because it would also hide my identity. Pulling on the uniform made me feel powerful and almost invincible.

I pulled the keycard out of my pocket and clipped it to the uniform, ensuring that it wouldn't be lost on the trek to the black site. I clipped a number of weapons onto my belt including a knife, a Taser, and a small handgun, ensuring it was fully loaded. I also grabbed a cell phone, one of a number of burners that Flint and Ashe had acquired and opened up the location tracking software. I put in the position of the compound and set out on my way. My movements were quick and sure as I traveled south. The compound was about four miles away and I jogged most of it, arriving just outside the barbed wire fence in about an hour. I powered down the burner when I closed in on it, using the brush to hide my advance. There wasn't a lot of it, and I stilled when I saw a guard walking around the perimeter with an identical uniform to the one that I was wearing.

I watched him as he strode around, his eyes glancing around for a moment before he stared back at the ground. I knew from the wolves' reconnaissance that the fence wasn't electrified so when I pressed my fingers against it, it reminded me of every other wired fence I'd ever come across. It was normal and had spots of rust but blended in well with the shrubbery. Some places were even covered with vines and I chose one of those to hide behind as I took a pair of wire cutters out from my pocket.

Quietly, I clipped through the fence, taking my time and making sure that I hid in a nearby ditch every time another guard came to walk the perimeter. This particular spot wasn't very visible, and it made cutting through the metal much easier because of it. I cut a door into the fence and peeled it open when the inside was unguarded, and then I squeezed myself past it. Quickly, I replaced the fence, ensuring that it appeared as though it had never been tampered with in the first place.

I meant to use it to escape from when I'd finished gathering the scientific intel I'd come for. I would slip in and out undetected, blending in with the rest of the humans that worked here until I found exactly what I wanted.

For the moment, this back section of the compound was abandoned, and I walked hurriedly to one of the windows in the back. I found it unlocked and pushed it open, climbing inside as silently as I could. I'd chosen this entryway specifically because it led into a storage room that was hardly used according to the camera footage I'd fast forwarded through last night. Quickly, I made my way to the front and pressed my ear to the door. I heard nothing and prepared myself to move on.

I slipped into the hallway unnoticed. Another guard walked by me and didn't say a word, but the walkie-talkie on his waist blurted out something about an incoming delivery. Nikita and her team would be on the back of that truck. I'd beaten them inside. I grinned, my face safely hidden behind the mask I was wearing and made my way through the building. With the uniform, I fit right into the guards patrolling the hallways and none of them gave me a second look. I was just a part of the scenery to those who worked here.

I passed by a number of men and women in suits, official-looking individuals who didn't care who I was or what I was doing. No one asked me for identification or what my job was because my disguise was the perfect ruse. I walked the halls and made my way down several stairwells until I came to the floor that the labs I'd observed were on. I wasn't stopped, not even once.

Here, men and women wore lab coats instead of suits. Some of them were even dressed in heavy personal protective equipment that reminded me of the biohazard suits I'd seen in the movies. It was around lunchtime and as I peered through the glass walls of the laboratories, I found that most of them were abandoned. I made my way inside and started to look through whatever I could find. There were lab notebooks on the counters and computers open and logged in along the back of each lab bay. I opened the nearest notebook I could find and flipped through, finding evidence of different compound structures and experiments in an effort to identify what made the betas go infertile. In another, I found differing information looking into what made the betas live for so long and what component of their biological system made them essentially immortal.

The scientists had gotten far in their research. I scanned through their data, looking at all the different sequencing they performed, along with spectrometry analysis of the protein structure and overexpression experiments they had performed. They had several ongoing aging experiments with mice where they'd extended their lifespan to almost double.

I took as many pictures as I could with the burner phone at my disposal. I lifted a USB drive off one of the nearby desks and copied all the data I could find off of the lab's internal servers. I stored a number of different samples in a thick packing container and poured some liquid nitrogen within it, ensuring that what I took wouldn't break down until I could put it in its proper storage conditions at the right temperatures they needed to be kept.

I'd be able to take this information and approach any pharmaceutical company with it. I'd be able to sell the information for the pack's gain and ensure we had plenty for the pack to live off of for the rest of our lives. We'd have enough funds to disappear out of the country and find somewhere safe to live. I'd be able to secure enough to ensure that the Department of Paranormal Activity never bothered my pack again.

When I was finished, I stood up and wandered down toward the end of the lab, and then I noticed a massive steel door that wasn't supposed to be there. It hadn't been on any of the blueprints that I'd studied. I scanned my keycard in front of it and it beeped once and then twice before it blinked green. The door slid open and I strode inside. What the heck was this?

I knew today was the weekend and nearly every lab I'd ever encountered had people working inside it no matter the time of day or week, but not this one. Nobody was inside. It was also extraordinarily clean in that every surface was organized and wiped down. All the bottles were labeled and dated. There was a single lab notebook on the bench, and I picked it up.

I opened it and started to read.

It belonged to a Dr. Richard Stevenson. He wasn't working on the immortality project, or the infertility one. He was working on something else entirely.

My mouth went dry.

He had been working on a genetic splicing project. He'd been taking the DNA from female beta embryos and combining it with human male genomes. This science wasn't for the good of mankind. This felt sinister.

The goal of his study was to create an entire race of wolf shifter super soldiers that the government would own, right down to the identifier written into their DNA. I licked my lips and took several pictures of the notebook, horrified at what I found. He'd created a number of fertilized embryos and incubated them to a point where they were living and breathing. He'd also taken several human males and treated them with a number of genetic modifiers that induced a partial wolf shift. His notes indicated that the changes were exceedingly painful for his specimens.

It was all strangely clinical. He never referred to the humans as anything other than his specimens. I lifted my head, hid the phone inside my uniform, and stared at a second doorway, wondering if that's where he kept the men and women he was testing on. There was a single computer and when I tapped the keyboard to turn it on, I found that it was locked. I turned away and approached the other door apprehensively when someone behind me cleared their throat.

"You're not supposed to be here. Your badge doesn't grant you access to this facility because it's outside of your jurisdiction, so that tells me that you're not a guard. The information contained in this lab is highly confidential and unfortunately for you, that means that you just signed your very own death warrant," a male voice said.

I stilled.

Fuck.

"Dr. Stevenson," I whispered, realizing it could be no one else.

"In the flesh," he answered.

I turned around to face him.

He was an older man, potentially in his late fifties. His

hair was mottled with white and gray, mixing with his natural dark chestnut color. His eyes were hard and unforgiving as he held up what appeared to be a small remote in his hand.

I reached for the gun at my waist and he shook his head as he clicked his tongue in annoyance.

"I wouldn't do that if I were you. Security is already on their way and not the type of security you're masquerading as. You see, you've stumbled on a secret study funded by the Department of Defense. It doesn't matter what you hear and see now though, because by the end of the day, you're going to be either in prison or, better yet, dead," he warned.

"You're not going to get away with this," I muttered.

He simply laughed. He chuckled at first, before it turned into a sinister bellow of laughter. I gritted my teeth and glared at him, and he laughed once more.

"You don't know the kind of people you're messing with, woman," he finally responded after he was able to get his amusement under control.

In less than a minute, a security team burst through the door, only all of them were carrying assault rifles, unlike the guards I'd been impersonating. All of them were rough and gritty and in that moment, I sincerely began to fear for my life. I'd gotten into something that I wasn't supposed to and now I was going to pay the price for it.

As Dr. Stevenson's men surrounded me, they roughly pulled my hands behind my back and strapped me in heavy handcuffs that I knew I'd be unable to break out of. Something hit me really hard in back of the head and my vision grew hazy.

I knew no more after that.

CHAPTER 8

Kiba

Capturing the delivery truck had been like taking candy from a baby. The hardest part had been getting the truck to stop, but all we had needed to do was push a fallen tree into the road, thereby making the path unpassable. There had only been the driver and a single guard, which left them incredibly unprepared for me and the combined strength of my pack. We'd taken the two men captive and tied them up to a tree after divesting them of all their clothes, leaving them completely naked. A few betas stayed behind to guard them.

Nikita had dressed the part of the driver while her brother Flint took the position of guard. Her team climbed into the back of the big rig while she and Flint took the head of the truck, readying themselves to drive and begin the most important part of their mission. I closed the back of the storage container behind them, whispering words of encouragement to the rest of the team hidden inside. Then we moved the log and cleared the road, allowing them to travel through the forest unhindered.

We followed about half a mile behind, under the cover of the brush at the side of the road. There had been no security patrolling the woods. It was all eerily quiet, and I got the feeling that things were going far too easily.

They'd gotten the truck into the black site compound almost effortlessly. The security guard at the gate had only checked Nikita's ID with hardly even a cursory glance. I watched the gate open and then close behind them, locking them inside as they pulled away to the receiving area where they'd use the truck as their own personal Trojan horse. We waited behind in case we were needed. We'd only head in if we were given the signal. If Nikita called for me, the rest of us would answer and create so much organized chaos that we'd break the betas out just like we'd done in the previous location. They were going to get out no matter what happened. I didn't care if the whole thing went quietly or not. I was going to free them, once and for all.

In the meantime, I found myself thinking of my mate, of the way her beautiful body molded to my own and of the soft whines that escaped her lips as I touched her and showed her that she would forever be mine in more ways than one. I could feel her heart beating, the tension of her nerves while she waited for me to return, and I smiled knowing what was to come after this was all over.

Out of habit, I sniffed the air and I could feel that she was close… much closer than she should be if she were actually where I'd told her to be right now. There was no way that she was back at base camp. She must have ignored my instructions and come here on her own.

Naughty girl. She was going to get spanked for that. Just thinking about her naked form over my knees made me hard and I found myself looking forward to putting her there and reddening her gorgeously bared backside. I couldn't wait to make her spread her thighs after I punished her, knowing that I'd find her soaking wet for me. After that, I'd make her beg for the privilege to come for me, over and over until there were tears running down her pretty cheeks.

Ever since I had found her and shown her that her place was naked by my side, our connection had only grown stronger. Our destinies were tied together as one and the magic of the earth was only serving to bring us even closer. Through that link, I could feel her worry, her joy, her pleasure, whatever she was feeling at any particular moment. I knew when she was missing home and her former life, and I did everything I could to ensure that I distracted her from those feelings whenever that happened.

Right now, though, there was a sliver of curiosity radiating from her. I wondered if she'd found something interesting, but then it suddenly changed to something far more sinister that made me stiffen immediately. I knew that something wasn't right.

I could feel her fear. It wasn't the type of fear that made her wet either. It was the kind of fear of being really, truly hurt. As the seconds passed, it transformed into the sort of terror that only the possibility of certain death could bring. She was in real danger and that was becoming clearer by the second. Her terror escalated and then it just vanished altogether, leaving me bereft and alone.

The moment my connection with her was severed, I knew something was very, very wrong. I had to get to her. Now.

"The omega is in danger. I must find her right away," I bellowed to my pack, using the silent connection between us all. *"You know what to do if Nikita needs you. I will return as soon as I can."*

The rest of my pack bowed their heads, knowing how incredibly important Dawn was to all of us. Without her, our kind would be in danger of extinction. Without her, there would be no children and there would be no us. I had to find her, and I had to do so right away.

I was going to do whatever it took to rescue her from whatever mess she'd gotten herself into.

When she was safe in my arms again, she was going to answer for her disobedience, and it was going to leave her very sore and very sorry by the time I finished wringing one painful climax after another from that beautiful little body. She would be pleading for mercy by the time I was done with her, but I wasn't going to stop until I decided that she'd had enough. She was going to learn that when it ended would never be up to her.

There would be time for that later.

I tore off into the woods, trying to use the connection between us to find her. It felt like it had gone black and the more I probed for it, the more I feared she might already be dead. I could smell that she was close, but I couldn't pinpoint her location, at least not from that alone. She wasn't back at base camp; she was here at the compound somewhere, and I was going to find her even if it killed me. I would do whatever it took to rescue my mate.

I stopped, lifted my snout into the breeze and took a long moment to inhale, searching for her. On the gentle breeze, I could smell her, and it gave me a direction to begin my search. I breathed a soft sigh of relief at that first clue. I had caught her sweet enticing scent and now I could follow it. It was faint, but it was there, and it was going to lead me straight to her.

Quickly, I circled around the compound in the dimming light of day, using the shadows to hide my massive wolf form. I followed her scent along the perimeter of the black site, eventually finding evidence of her presence by a dilapidated corner of the fence, where there was a single strand of her hair caught in the welded connections of the metal. She'd been here. That was clear as day. There was no evidence of anyone else there either. She'd snuck inside all on her own.

I made a decision then.

When I finally got my hands on her, I was going to punish that delightful little bottom of hers with my cock too after I finished thoroughly reddening it with my palm.

I nudged the fence with my snout, taking note of the fresh cuts in the wires that indicated that she'd clipped her way through. I growled softly and followed her scent, careful to crouch close to the ground and hide whenever anyone drew near. I made sure to avoid the cameras watching the area surrounding the building. There was a single guard walking the perimeter of the fence, who proved fairly simple to avoid. He walked quite slowly and didn't pay much attention to anything inside the compound. Surprisingly, he was more concerned with tapping something on his cell phone rather than looking around him. Apparently, things never got very exciting out here in the woods, or at least they didn't on his watch. They were going to today though. I was going to make sure of it because my mate was in danger.

Where the hell had she gone?

When the guard had passed, I followed Dawn's scent to a window that was slightly ajar. She'd gone inside all alone without the protection of the pack or anyone else. I peeked inside, seeing a storage room with several boxes stacked on top of a bunch of shelving units. It didn't seem to be occupied at all, nor did it seem to be particularly well used due to the thick layers of dust on the shelves. I was just about to nudge the window back open and climb inside myself, when the sound of a door opening around the corner drew my attention. I stilled and my ears perked up, hearing the quiet crackle of leaves breaking under footfalls. I turned away from the window and pressed my paws back down into the earth, stalking along the wall of the building until I could peek around to see what was happening just around the corner.

A group of men had exited through a door and were climbing into a large black SUV. They were wearing heavy combat gear, much thicker and higher tech than any of the guards that I'd seen walking the perimeter of the compound so far. None of them said a word and then another man walked up behind them, only he had a small, feminine form slung over his shoulder. I swallowed a growl when I saw her. It was my Dawn. I'd know that beautiful little body anywhere, even if she was all dressed up in the same garb that the security detail that worked here typically wore.

How the hell had she gotten one of their uniforms?

She wasn't moving. Her limbs were lax and when I sniffed the air, I could smell the copper scent of blood wafting toward me. Her blood.

Fucking bastards. I was going to tear apart whoever had hurt her.

I studied her more closely, noticing that her hair was matted at the back of her scalp. They'd hit her in the head, knocking her out from behind.

I growled, the sound low and ominous. The man carrying my mate looked in my direction and narrowed his eyes. There was recognition there. He knew what I was. There was a yellow flash in his gaze, and I paused.

I'd seen that before, only stronger and in the eyes of my betas. These weren't members of my pack though. These weren't my wolf shifters. These men were something else entirely.

The man rolled his upper lip, snarling at me, challenging me. There was no way I was going to back down now, not when he had my mate. I growled louder and he didn't flinch as he should have. I was the alpha and that brought with it a certain power. If I was ever displeased or had to subdue a member of my pack, my growl would be more than enough to pin them to the ground. They'd be unable to fight back against the power of the natural order until I released them from it.

This man didn't respond to any of that.

He appeared human, but there was something more than that. Something wild, untamable, and entirely too dangerous, unnatural even. The longer I stared at him, the more I felt like something was undeniably wrong.

The rest of the men turned toward me and the one carrying Dawn passed her off to another. He moved quickly, tossing her in the back of the SUV and hopping into the driver's seat as fast as he could. The engine revved and I raced forward to try to stop him, but the others barked several quick orders. They turned toward me and prepared themselves to fight, blocking my path to the vehicle as it sped away down the road toward the gate.

They weren't ready for me. I was the alpha and that made me the ultimate predator. The men reached for the guns at their waists, but I had already begun to move. My claws tore into the ground, propelling my body forward toward the men. One of them managed to pull a semi-automatic from the holster. He popped off a shot and it went off in some wild direction, thudding into a nearby tree instead of me. I growled loudly and behind me, angry snarls echoed at my back.

My pack had come. They were here to battle by my side.

We would get our omega back, together.

They howled behind me, furious as the SUV peeled off behind the human men. My wolves moved to follow but the team fired off a number of warning shots. One bullet grazed my paw and it burned hot. I snarled in pain as I realized what had happened.

They had silver bullets. They knew our weakness.

This was trouble.

I paused, furious.

"They have silver weapons," I snarled. *"Be wary. Circle around and do not engage unless you are close enough to take one of them down in a single blow."*

A number of wolves stood at my back. Rebecca was one of them.

"I will not leave your side, alpha. The omega is important to me too," she snarled next to me, furious at what she'd seen so far.

"I will not see you hurt, beta," I replied harshly, and I could see her shudder at the gravity of my tone.

"I'm not going to be," she growled in return, and she crouched low to the ground, gathering her strength for the opportune moment to strike. The men spread outward into a pointed formation, training their weapons upon us and readying themselves to fire.

Their irises were even more yellow then before, almost as if they were changing right before me. They had seemingly grown in size, filling out their combat gear even more than when I'd first laid eyes on them. I studied them more closely now, noticing that their beards seemed thicker, their noses longer, their nails sharper.

They smelled distinctly of human but there was a very faint scent of wolf there. It felt like it didn't belong together.

I rolled my upper lip when the man in charge took a step toward me. He was careful to keep his gun aimed directly at my head. I took a step forward in challenge and he faltered just the slightest bit. I growled more loudly this time and a glimmer of fear crossed his features. He was scared and rightly so. Even though they were carrying silver bullets and weren't entirely human, I was the alpha wolf and that carried with it a certain invincibility that none of the other shifters were privy to.

Sure, silver was fatal to me, just like it was to my betas. There was one very important difference for me though. It took time and quite a bit of it to really hurt me. Eventually, it could take me down, but it would take a lot. A whole lot.

He'd have to empty that entire clip into me before I was able to reach him and rip his head from his shoulders. The likelihood of that was slim to none. I crouched, readying myself to attack. Beside me, Rebecca trembled with eagerness. She wanted to fight, and I did too. The others were restless just like the two of us.

"I don't want to lose any wolves today," I said carefully to them.

"Our lives are yours, alpha. For the omega," they all replied in unison.

"For the omega," I echoed. *"Wait for my word."*

I could feel the presence of my betas moving into position in the nearby woods, using the cover of the brush to hide their coats while the men's attention was kept focused on me and the small group of wolves at my back. A second segment of my pack was circling around the soldiers, closing in on them from behind. Like a vise, we would close in on them from the front and the back until they were no more. They'd taken my mate and they were going to pay for that with their lives.

"Hold," I ordered.

My wolves tensed, preparing themselves.

The soldiers stilled, watching us closely with a sense of confidence that I couldn't wait to destroy.

"Hold," I said once more. My betas moved in behind the men. They were so close that I could see the golden glimmer of their eyes amongst the dense brush.

I took a single step forward, wanting to test the soldiers.

All at once, the front line of men shrieked, a sound that reminded me of the yip of a young pup. In a flurry, I watched as they shifted right in front of me. I narrowed my eyes as I took in the sight of their bodies transforming, their fingers elongating and their nails lengthening into long claws. Their fur wasn't as thick as ours though and their front paws didn't descend all the way down to touch the ground. Instead, they remained upright on two feet.

Their snouts were elongated. Their ears were pointed as ours were, but they didn't turn into full wolves. Instead, there were elements of both human and wolves, as well as the presence of certain features that were distinctly werewolf in origin. It was as though someone had taken features from each of those three beasts and mixed them together as one.

I snarled.

These weren't men. They weren't shifter or werewolves either. These were monsters. Genetically engineered soldiers designed to fight for the people who ran this place. If I was a gambling man, I'd bet that they were created right here in a lab deep underground and I'd also wager that was exactly what Dawn had found before she'd been discovered and taken from me.

The hideous monsters growled in return, holding the front line while a number of men still pointed guns at us stood in back of them.

My betas were in full position behind them.

"Those in the woods, take out the humans with the guns first. We will deal with the beasts," I ordered. *"Hold for a moment longer. You will attack on my word."*

"Yes, alpha," my pack responded as one.

The engineered beasts dug at the dirt with their claws, ready for battle. They had no idea what was coming for them though. My pack was strong, and these monsters were going to find out exactly how fierce and tough we were, even if they had silver bullets.

"*Now.*"

The clearing exploded into a flurry of fur, claws, and bullets. My betas tore in from their positions in the woods behind them and attacked the men holding the back line, ripping into wrists and throats without pause while I and the others burst forward toward the beasts at the front. Our attack surrounded them in moments and the look in their eyes went wild. The sound of men screaming echoed as we shredded into their numbers, but I heard the distinct yelp of my betas in pain too. Our attack had not gone without sacrifice.

We fought onward. One of the monsters and I slammed into each other, while he tried to use his claws to tear into my flesh. He failed though. His claws weren't going to slash at me, not ever. I used his momentary surprise at his botched attack and used my full body weight to slam him down to the ground hard. Without hesitation, I pressed myself onto him, biting into his throat and tearing through his jugular vein with my teeth. Blood spurted into my mouth and onto the dirt around me, but I didn't care.

I moved onto the next. Quickly.

My pack worked in concert, taking out one man after the next. The copper scent of blood hung heavy on the air as we decimated their numbers. We ripped each one apart, limb by limb, until all their guns fell to the earth.

A shrill alarm began to ring, so loud that it made my ears flatten to my head.

More men poured out of the building, exiting through the same door that they'd carried Dawn out of. These men had a similar scent to the soldiers we'd already encountered, although it was weaker. The men were large, and though they appeared quite strong, they were no match for us.

My pack took care of them as though their deaths were simply child's play.

After all that was over, a single man strode out from that door. He was bigger than all the rest and he had his gaze trained right on me. He was older, with long white hair and eyes flecked with yellow. He was wearing a pristine white lab coat and the hair on the back of my neck rose in alarm.

His scent was different. Stronger. More intense. He smelled of human and wolf and werewolf in a combination that was much more potent than the rest. It felt instinctually more dangerous than the men that we had already faced.

"I take it that you're the leader," he observed.

I growled low, warning the man that he was skating on thin ice. I wouldn't hesitate to rip out his throat just as I had done to the abominations behind me. I had to end this and soon. The more time that passed, the farther away that black SUV would travel and the harder it would be to get my mate back.

"I'm going to take you alive. You would be the final ingredient for my perfect soldier. Your DNA is the answer that I've been waiting for. I'm sure of it," the man whispered. His eyes opened just a hair too wide and I got the distinct impression that this man was insane.

"This one is mine," I told my betas.

They continued to fight, taking down the rest of the men who had joined this one. They circled around me in a wide ring, using their presence simply to intimidate this man who had challenged their alpha.

"My work will be complete when I have your samples. You'll make me famous," the man whispered, his voice breaking with a distinctly unhinged tremor. His gaze remained trained on me, a certain deranged madness behind those wide eyes. He reached into the pocket of his lab coat and pulled out what looked like a small dart gun. Without hesitation, he aimed at me and engaged the trigger. Instinctively, I rolled to the side and the feathered dart landed in the dirt, directly in the spot where I'd been standing before.

His upper lip rolled and the feral insanity in his eyes intensified into fury. In a rush, his clothes were torn into shreds as his body increased in size, his muscles ripping through the threads of cloth as though they were sheets of paper. His canines and his claws lengthened, as did the thickness of his white hair. Coarse fur sprouted through his pale skin and he roared as he stared me down. His wolf features were stronger, but there were still elements of werewolf in his makeup. He still stood upright at nearly eight feet tall, long arms and legs flexing as he readied himself to attack. While his fur was denser than the others had been, it was still stringy and not nearly as thick as mine. His irises were flecked with both golden yellow and bright red. They were the eyes of an overzealous madman.

He burst toward me, his movement brash. I reared up on my hind legs and snarled as his body collided with mine, but I was still bigger and stronger. I was the top predator here on Earth, the ultimate design in natural perfection. Even with all his engineered traits, he would still end up being no match for me.

His insanity brought with it a certain ferocity though that made him the fiercest competition that I'd ever encountered thus far. I roared as he bit at my flesh, his sharp canines hard enough to just puncture through my skin. The sound of my growls thundered through the forest, deeper and far more ominous than his. My betas yipped and barked, having destroyed what was left of the soldiers.

Now they were watching me and cheering me on.

The ultimate showdown had begun. They knew better than to intervene. This was between me and this mad scientist.

My claws tore at him, our bodies tangled together as we fought. My movements were more precise and each time I bit at him or used my body to throw him to the ground, it started becoming more and more clear that I was the stronger out of the two of us. Almost imperceptibly, his kicks and punches began to weaken, and I began to take advantage of that. Using my entire weight, I threw him backwards and he stumbled, slamming into a tree directly behind him. The sound of his skull cracking against the trunk was sickeningly loud and the scent of his mutant blood was a bitter tang on the air.

He looked dazed for a long moment and I acted swiftly, throwing myself into him again and knocking his head against the tree once more. His eyes rolled back into his head for a second before he grinned in my direction, his crooked teeth reminding me of a rabid hyena. He screamed, the sound high pitched and eerie. In a last-ditch effort, he sprinted right at me, but I was ready for him.

I leapt up, using every ounce of my strength to propel myself off the ground. I opened my jaws and roared, colliding with him with full force. My front paws slammed into his chest and knocked him to the ground. I didn't hesitate, not even for a moment. I ripped into his throat using every single bit of my strength. I tasted mutant flesh and blood, but I didn't stop.

Not until he stopped moving. Not until he was dead beneath me.

When I was finally sure it was over, I pushed myself off of him and stared out at my pack. The alarm was still blaring, and Nikita's voice echoed in my head.

"They know we're here and security is on lockdown. We've managed to open the gate, but we're going to need help," she told me.

"The pack will answer," I replied. I looked out at the wolves

surrounding me, looking to their leader for direction. *"Three of you will come with me. The four of us will rescue the omega and then we will return to help the others and ensure that the rest of the pack is set free."*

"I will come with you," Rebecca volunteered, stepping forward and boldly leveling her gaze at me. Two other wolves moved by her side and I nodded. There was no time to be selective. We had to move.

"Let's go. To the rest of you, let chaos become you," I ordered, and my pack scattered, leaving me, Rebecca, and the other two volunteers, Luna and Jack.

I burst forward, sprinting down the dirt road and following the tracks that the SUV had left behind. We ran hard and fast in silence, knowing that time was of the essence. In less than ten minutes, I could hear the gentle rumble of the vehicle up ahead. It could only move so fast on this uneven terrain and we could run faster.

The four of us ran together and once we caught sight of the car, we moved outward in a rectangular formation. Knowing that my mate was inside that vehicle fueled me to run even harder than before and once I reached the driver's side door, I leapt forward and sank my teeth into the front tire. I pulled away as quickly as I had bitten it, watching as the wheel began to deflate. The air escaping through the holes let out a high-pitched whooshing sound and my wolves followed suit with the other three tires.

The SUV shook dangerously, and I leapt up, slamming down onto the hood of the car. The metal crushed under my weight and it nose-dived into the ground, screeching to a halt as the car embedded its front end into the dirt road. The groan of twisting metal was deafening as it finally came to a complete stop and the ensuing silence felt just as loud. I turned my head, staring into the windshield at the two soldiers inside and the looks of terror on their faces were in stark contrast to the false arrogance that had been there when they'd sped away with my mate.

Luna and Jack guarded each door while Rebecca shifted back into her human form, opening the back and reaching inside for Dawn. She lifted my mate's small body from the seat and strode away a good distance, looking to me for instruction as to what to do next.

Dawn was entirely still.

I bounded off the car and shifted myself, leaping toward Rebecca and my mate's motionless body. I took her into my arms, breathing a sigh of relief as I watched her ribcage move with the timing of her breath. She was still alive. I pressed a kiss to the center of her forehead and she finally moved a little bit, groaning quietly as she did so.

Her eyes fluttered open and met mine. She was still slightly dazed and out of it, but as she blinked, they slowly cleared.

"You're in a lot of trouble, little omega," I whispered, and her lips opened just slightly in recognition of the meaning of my words.

"Kiba," she whispered, her small form curling into my arms. I brushed my palm against the back of her head, feeling the dried blood in her hair. None of it appeared to be fresh, indicating that the wound had closed at least. It had left a healthy bump on the back of her head though, which was likely very sore.

"How do you feel, sweet mate?" I asked her softly, taking any and all threat out of my voice. I was just happy to see that she was alive and that she was now safe in my arms once more. Now was not the time to deal with her disobedience. There would plenty more of that later after we successfully freed the rest of the betas.

"I've got a nasty headache," she murmured. "But it could be worse, I suppose."

I nuzzled my forehead into her shoulder.

"I'm so relieved that you're okay," I said quietly.

"I'm sorry I worried you," she answered, hiding her face in my shoulder.

"I know. We'll handle that when the time comes, but there are more important matters at hand right now, aren't there, little mate," I replied calmly, lifting her chin with my finger and making her look at me.

"Yes, alpha," she whispered softly.

"Good girl. Can you stand and climb up on my back?" I asked her, knowing that the rest of my betas were awaiting my return at the black site.

"I think so," she answered, and I carefully helped her climb to her feet. She moved rather sluggishly as she found her footing and I hesitated, watching her closely.

"You're not going to leave my side until I give you permission, little mate," I said protectively. She blinked several times and her expression looked less pained as more time went on.

"I understand," she replied quietly, lifting her eyes to mine.

"Good. Take your time. We won't return until you're ready," I instructed, and she nodded. I shifted beside her and she leaned against me, pressing her forehead into my side for several long minutes as she gathered herself. She finally took a deep breath and pushed herself away from me. I knelt down and she slowly climbed onto my back.

"Hold on tight, little mate. I got you," I told her.

"I know you do," she whispered quietly into my ear.

My heart beat again and again. For her. Only for her.

CHAPTER 9

Dawn

I CLUNG to his back like a lifeline as Kiba pounded through the forest, back to the black site where the rest of the pack was waiting for him. He ran a bit more slowly than usual, making sure to check in with me from time to time to make sure that I was still alright. My ears still rang from the blow to the back of my head and my vision still wavered occasionally. I touched the bump that had been left behind and found that my hair was matted with dried blood. I bit my lip and pressed my forehead into the place between his shoulders, feeling the gentle but painful pounding in my head from it. It was gradually fading, but it still hurt quite a bit.

The journey back to the compound was surprisingly short. I don't know how long I'd been knocked out for, but it didn't really matter. When we got back, the alarms were blaring and wolves were running back and forth, locked in combat with human guards. Kiba took me in through the back and I saw the remains of a fight that had already taken place.

I sucked in a breath at the carnage, taking in the mutant-looking creatures with their thin fur and gangly limbs spread out all over the ground, pale and lifeless. Many of them were in pieces.

"They'd taken you from me and they had to answer for it," Kiba's voice rang out in my head. I nodded into his shoulder, staying silent on top of him. I peered around, watching as he held back, and the others ran into the fray.

"We need help at the lower levels. The guards have come together to hold the lower entrance and are blocking the way to the beta enclosures," Nikita called out and Kiba growled, the sound low and quiet. All the wolves around us perked up their ears and gathered together around their alpha.

"Then kill them."

"Wait, you don't have to do that," I rushed to say, and he was silent. "Let me help. I know a way in," I offered quietly.

Kiba grunted with displeasure.

"There is a lab down below, another entrance into where the betas were being kept prisoner. It wasn't on the blueprints," I quickly explained. "Let me lead you there and we can break out the betas without the guards finding out." I knew the layout of that floor now and I was the only one who did. Without me, they wouldn't be able to get out without killing everyone in the way.

Kiba was silent for a long moment, likely considering my words. I knew he didn't enjoy killing anyone. He'd gone out of his way to make sure very few people died at the black site I'd been assigned to conduct research in and even in the planning of today's mission, he'd been adamant about wanting to avoid killing humans.

"If we do this, you will not leave my side. If you do, I will not hesitate to take you over my knee right then and there to remind you who is the alpha and that will only preface the real punishment that you would get later. Do you understand me, mate?" he warned carefully.

I shivered, still sitting atop his back. My pussy clenched tightly, and my mouth went dry. I already knew I was in trouble for breaking into the compound on my own. I had no desire to make it any worse.

"Yes, alpha," I responded quietly, my voice subdued. I wouldn't fight him, and I didn't want to. I had been extremely relieved that I had opened my eyes to find that he had rescued me, instead of finding myself in some derelict prison in some government facility or worse. I was safe in his arms and even if that meant I was going to be punished for what I had done, it left me with a sense of security and relief to be with him again.

"Now, make me proud and lead us," he said after that, his voice cool and collected. He was a true leader, knowing when to claim the lead and when to allow others to take it for themselves. I was proud to call him my alpha. He knelt down and allowed me to climb off his back. I walked around the building, looking for the storage room I'd entered through before. It wasn't far. I pushed open the window all the way this time and climbed inside. Kiba and a number of wolves followed behind me. Together, we made our way through the compound, finding most of the hallways abandoned and unguarded, which led me to believe that they were deeper in the lower levels. The alarm continued to blare loud over the speakers, but I did my best to ignore it.

I retraced my steps until I reached the more central area, deciding to use the lesser used service stairwells this time so that we wouldn't run into anyone else. The wolves' paws were silent on the floor as we walked, and I did my best to keep the sound of my boots as quiet as I could. We descended until I reached the laboratory area, leading them back through the metal door that I'd found earlier that day. The lab was abandoned now and in quite a bit more disarray than it had been before.

I hadn't gone through the other door in here, but I would bet that it led right to the captive betas. I grabbed the metal doorknob and twisted it.

"I can feel them. My betas are close," Kiba's voice said quietly in my head.

Turns out I was right.

As soon as I opened the door, the betas began to howl. Their alpha had come for them. They were all in individual cages made of clear bulletproof glass and as soon as Kiba walked in, they began throwing their bodies against the walls that held them. There was a lanyard just to the right of the door with a keycard and when I picked it up, I realized that it had been Dr. Stevenson's. I rushed forward and pressed it against the closest cage and the door slid open. In a hurry, I moved onto the next and the next, freeing more than two dozen different betas in less than a minute. Once they were all out, I turned back to Kiba and he nodded in my direction.

"Good work, my sweet omega," he said proudly, and I couldn't help myself as I smiled in return. *"Retreat, Nikita. The betas are with me now."*

She didn't ask questions. Instead, she simply relayed the order and the entire pack began to move out. I jumped up on Kiba's back once more and we left the same way we had come in. We didn't run into any more guards, likely due to the fact that Ashe was replaying old camera footage over and over to their systems in order to cover our tracks. We slipped out of the building with ease and before I knew it, we'd made it back to the back to the portion of the fence that I had cut through. I leapt down off of Kiba and crawled through, while the others followed.

"Up."

Once more, I climbed up onto my alpha's back and the pack sprinted off into the forest, using the shadows of the falling night to hide their escape.

* * *

The next several days were spent putting as much distance between the pack and the black site as possible. I ate berries along the way as a snack and a hearty meal of meat cooked over the fire from whatever the wolves hunted and caught for me that day. Finally, Kiba announced that we'd gone far enough, and the pack cheered with delight, knowing that they could settle down and rest. During that time, I'd fully recovered from my ordeal and the bump at the back of my head had gone away entirely. The cut healed quickly, not even leaving a scar.

One afternoon shortly thereafter, the two of us were sitting by the fire when I felt his mood change to something darker and far more dangerous.

Kiba shifted into his human form for the first time in days, and I licked my lips, taking a long moment to admire his chiseled and naked body. His chest rippled as he stared at me and I had the sudden feeling that I was in a great deal of trouble. My nipples peaked and my pussy clenched as I sat there, still fully covered by the guard outfit I had stolen. He'd hinted at the fact that I'd earned a punishment before, so I knew it was coming. His dark eyes appraised me thoughtfully and I knew that time was now. I swallowed nervously and waited for what would come next.

"We have something to talk about, don't we, little mate?" he began, and a shiver raced down my spine. There was something about the way he'd said those words that made me feel small and vulnerable and entirely too much like a naughty little girl. I bit my lip and curled my arms around my shoulders, feeling my thighs tremble with nervous anticipation.

"Yes, alpha," I whispered, my voice quiet. Submissive.

"You put the entire pack in danger by going off on your own, my sweet mate. I want you to explain to me why you disobeyed my instructions," he continued, his voice far too calm and too collected. It made me even more anxious for what I knew was about to happen.

He was going to punish me.

In a small voice, I told him why I had done it, why I'd broken into the lab to steal the data and how I planned to use it to set up the pack with the funds to remain safe for a long time. That I hadn't gone in on a whim. That I'd disobeyed for a reason.

"The pack is my family now, sir," I said softly, dropping my eyes. "I just wanted to help."

"I'm so very proud of you, my little mate," he responded, before he moved closer to me. His palm caressed the side of my cheek and I pressed myself into him, enjoying his gentleness for the time being. "You should have told me your plan and I would have made sure that you had adequate protection by your side, but you didn't, and you were ambushed as a result. Do you know how afraid I was when our connection was severed? I couldn't tell if you were alive or dead and that terrified me, sweet girl."

His words made me feel even smaller even though they were gentle. He didn't yell at me or tell me that he was disappointed in me. Instead, he kept his hand against my cheek and pulled me close to his chest. I breathed in his woodsy masculine scent and it gave me comfort, despite the anxiety cascading through me at the prospect of what he was going to do to me.

"I'm sorry," I whispered.

"I know you are, sweet mate, but you're going to have to answer for your disobedience, aren't you?"

"Yes, alpha," I whimpered. Even though I was afraid, my pussy clenched tightly, and I knew that I was wet. He held me for a long moment with those strong arms, before he eventually lifted my chin with a single finger and forced me to look straight into his eyes.

"Strip," he commanded.

I let out a small cry as a jolt of pleasure raced straight down to my core. I wasn't sure what was about to happen, but I knew by the end of it that I would be sore in more ways than one.

Slowly, I began with the belt at my waist. I slid the leather through the clasp and then pulled it free from the loops of my black pants. Kiba held out one hand expectantly and I hesitantly placed my belt in his palm. I froze as I watched him fold it over and snap it together, the sound loud amidst the quiet of the afternoon breeze. I was suddenly keenly aware of the fact that we weren't alone, that we were right next to the central campfire and that the members of the pack were all around us.

"Can't we go off into the woods? Just me and you?" I whispered nervously.

"No. Your punishment is going to take place right here, little omega, to remind you of your place in this pack," he answered firmly, and I knew better than to say anything more. I shivered, feeling my pussy tighten hard knowing I was probably going to be put over his knee in front of the entire group.

The fire crackled beside us and I reached for the hem of my t-shirt before I lifted it over my head. Having to bare myself like this felt utterly shameful and so very naughty, but I knew that I didn't have a choice whether I wanted to or not. I unbuttoned my pants next and pushed them down over my hips. The guard uniform hadn't had a bra or panties with it, so I'd gone naked beneath it.

"Hands on your head," he instructed.

I stood entirely naked now in nothing but a pair of boots. I could feel my body trembling before him. I shook even harder as he reached for me, trailing his fingertips across my breasts and I sucked in an anxious breath. His fingers loosely tightened around my nipples and my chest rose and fell with nervousness. Hesitantly, I pressed my own fingers to the back of my scalp, doing my best to try to be obedient for him even though I feared what was about to happen. My heartbeat went wild in my chest, hammering hard as I waited for the first bite of pain.

He pinched my nipples lightly once and then more firmly, so that a slight pinch burst across my breasts. The air escaped my lungs in a single shocked rush, and I pressed my lips together so that I didn't cry out, so that everyone else couldn't hear how very afraid I felt.

He twisted my nipples hard and I couldn't stop myself from pitching forward, but he didn't let me fall. Instead, he used his shoulder to catch me while he punished my breasts, pinching them harshly enough to make me whimper in pain.

"Your bottom is going to be very sore by the time I'm through with you, little mate. You're earned quite the punishment and you're going to take all of it, aren't you?" he said softly, so that only I could hear.

"Yes, sir," I whispered, my voice shaking with uneasiness.

He gripped my upper arm roughly, bringing me down with him as he sat down on a fallen log a short distance away from the fire. I landed over his knees with my bottom completely bared and on display. I moaned with shame. His fingers caressed the backs of my thighs before they slid in between them. His fingertips glided along my wetness and I whimpered with desire. They slipped forward to circle my clit and I couldn't help myself as I lifted my hips for him. I wondered if he was going to allow me to come for him. I hoped that he would.

Without warning, his palm slapped down hard on my naked backside. I keened at the unexpected sting and then it happened again. And then again. There was no time to get used to the harsh bite of each spank. The only thing I could do was take it. I lifted my head and I could see the others watching me getting a spanking over my alpha's knee. I was naked and they were witnessing every last shameful slap. The crack of his palm against my bared skin was loud and each one made me feel even smaller and more vulnerable than before, especially because I knew the others were seeing the whole thing too.

Kiba was going to teach me a lesson tonight and I had a feeling it was going to be a hard one. I slowly realized that being punished like this in front of everyone was an incredibly sobering and effective way to bring that very lesson home. Even despite it all, I was horrified to discover that I was still unbelievably wet, even more so than before.

The spanking became hard and fast. I tried to twist and turn my hips to avoid the harshness of his palm, but when he started punishing my thighs instead, I had even more difficulty holding myself together. I cried out as my thighs splayed and his fingers cracked against the edges of my pussy folds. I tried to remain still. It was hard because it hurt so very much. He forcibly spread my legs open then and cracked several fingers against my wet pussy, spanking it much harder than I had anticipated.

I tried to keep control. I attempted to keep my body still despite the scalding ache that was radiating across my bared flesh. My breath hitched and I breathed in deep, trying to remain calm despite the terrible sting that he was branding into my bottom. It was so hard though. This was a very real punishment and I knew that there still was so much more to come.

He spanked my pussy several more times before he returned to my backside, taking his time to thoroughly punish my thighs too. Those hurt the worst and I struggled to take each one. My cries echoed off the trees. There was no discussion amongst the pack tonight. Instead, they were silent, and I feared that every single pair of eyes was trained on the reddening of my disobedient backside over my alpha's knee. When I lifted my head, I knew that they were. They were watching their leader put his mate thoroughly in her place.

My pussy clenched hard and I could feel my wetness trickling down my inner thighs. There was little doubt in my mind that Kiba could see it too and that the light of the fire would reflect off of it as well, giving away my arousal to the rest of the pack.

Kiba spanked me hard, giving me no mercy in my punishment. The sting was harsh, the pain vivid, and I struggled to take it. My thighs shook and I cried out, my sounds of struggle slowly getting louder and louder. Even though I attempted to keep myself quiet, I soon realized that I wasn't going to be able to.

Kiba was making sure of it.

"Please, alpha," I begged. "I won't disobey you again."

"You've got a very thorough punishment coming, little mate. It's far from over and I think you know that, don't you?"

"Yes, sir," I whimpered. I knew the truth of his words. I knew that this spanking was just the start of what was to come. I also knew that it wasn't going to end until I was sobbing for him, whether it was from orgasms or the belt, I didn't yet know.

He paused the spanking for a moment and gripped my

bottom cheeks with his fingers. I gasped as he spread my ass, displaying me in a way that I had never been exposed before. No one had ever looked at me like this before and even as a harsh jolt of shame careened through me, an even stronger quiver of desire raced straight down to my needy pussy. I could feel my muscles tighten with arousal and I foolishly hoped that my punishment was over, that he would allow me to come for him now.

I was wrong.

His fingers pressed up against my wetness and he slowly inserted a finger into my pussy, once and then twice, before he dragged it backwards. My mind went blank.

He couldn't. No. Not there. No one had ever touched me there.

It was wrong. It was dirty. It was far more arousing than it should have been.

His fingertip rested against my bottom hole, a silent ominous threat that he could take me there if he wanted to.

"I'm sorry," I pleaded, trying to stop the inevitable.

That same finger pushed against my reluctant hole, just enough to show me that he could. I stilled, not knowing what to do. My thighs trembled as I nervously waited for what he would do next. He increased the pressure of that digit and I whimpered, feeling a very deep sense of shame and arousal that he was doing this to me in front of everyone else.

My disobedience had cost me. Earning his forgiveness was going to be far more than I had bargained for and it was going to hurt in ways that I could never have foreseen.

That finger breached into my bottom and I cried out at the burning pinch of pain as he stretched my tight hole for the very first time. I couldn't control myself as my thighs trembled from the confusing sensations coursing through my body. My pussy spasmed with need. Pain and pleasure molded into one and it became difficult to tell one from the other. It soon became one intoxicating sensation and I moaned as it quickly overwhelmed me.

"I'm sorry, sir. I'm sorry," I whimpered.

"I know you are, little mate," he answered gently as he pushed his finger deeper into my bottom. I felt humbled and subdued by this more than anything else he had ever done to me, including the spankings and the switching he'd given me when we'd first met.

"I want you to remember this moment, omega. I am your alpha and you will do as I say. You will obey me and when you are disobedient, you will be very thoroughly punished. Do you understand me?"

"Yes, alpha," I whimpered.

"You listen much better when my finger is in your tight little bottom, don't you?"

I shuddered and a quiet cry escaped my lips.

"Answer me, omega."

"Yes, sir," I whispered, as my pussy quivered with need.

With one finger still inside my bottom, he caressed my wet folds with the others. Those digits slid along my moist flesh and I was thankful for the curtain of my hair that was hiding my shame.

"It makes you very wet to be punished this way, doesn't it, omega?"

"Yes, sir," I said softly, fruitlessly trying to control my body from reacting to his fierce dominance.

He added a second finger then. He wasn't gentle.

I cried out from the burning pain and he pumped those digits in and out of my bottom. It hurt far more than I anticipated, and the ache hurtled up and down my spine. The pain was more intense at first, a cruel reminder that this was still a punishment. As it began to fade, I was left with a very deep sense of shame because it was making me very wet.

He was right. This was turning me on, and I didn't know

why. It felt naughty and wrong, but at the same time it was so incredibly arousing. It left me feeling needy and more than ever, it reminded me that I wasn't in control. He was and he could touch me wherever he wanted, whenever he wanted, including my virgin bottom hole.

"I want you to think about something. Right now, I have two fingers inside your tight little bottom. Before your punishment is over, my cock is going to be here instead. You're going to come with my cock inside your bottom and you're going to do it with the entire pack watching you. You're going to come until there's tears streaming down your cheeks, omega, and you're not going to stop until I say you've had enough," he warned.

My breath caught in my throat.

He couldn't.

I started to beg. I pleaded for him to reconsider. I told him I was sorry, over and over again, but he ignored me. Instead, he removed his fingers from my bottom and grasped me around the waist. He lifted me up and deposited me over a fallen log. I watched with nervous fear as he picked up the thick black leather belt he'd put aside.

I could still feel the ache from his touch all over my bottom hole. My flesh stung from his palm and now I nervously waited for my spanking to begin with my very own belt. The terrible leather swung back and forth, an extremely menacing warning of what was to come.

He ignored my pleas. I had known he would. He laid that belt across my bare backside, its cool caress haunting and intimidating, and I feared him in that moment.

The first stroke from that belt was like a bolt of lightning searing into my flesh. It burned hot as fire and the air rushed out of my lungs in a single breath. I struggled to draw in another as the belt whipped against my naked ass once more.

The switching he'd given me before had been harsh, but it

was nothing like this. This was far more intense, brutal even and there was nothing I could do but take it. I felt helpless and when the belt fell again, my breath hitched in my throat.

I had a feeling that this was going to break me.

Little did I know just how much it would.

He whipped me hard with that belt, over and over until I was sure that my entire bottom was welted from it. My fingers dug into the log, trying to hold on and keep myself from reaching backwards to stop him. The pace of the thrashing slowly increased, and I felt myself losing more and more control until the first tear rolled down my cheek.

Then I lost it all.

One tear fell after the next until they dripped off my chin down into the dirt below. The belt didn't stop, nor did it slow down, welting my backside again and again as it hammered in the message that he would always be the alpha and I, the omega.

He was in charge. I wasn't.

He whipped my naked bottom until I was sobbing and then he thrashed it some more. By the time he finally stopped, I was a bawling mess of tears and apologies and even then, I knew it wasn't over.

He laid my shirt on the log beside me, before he lifted me up off of it and placed me on my back. He took the end of the belt and snapped it against my pussy, not even giving me the chance to prepare myself for its awful sting. I cried out and my thighs instinctively tried to close, but his hand prevented that from happening so that he could whip my poor little pussy with that awful piece of leather. He didn't stop there though. He used that same leather hide to whip both of my nipples, one after the other in quick succession and I yelped in surprise, unable to defend myself. When my hands came down to cover my breasts, he grabbed at my wrists. Then he used a long vine to bind them together before he tied it above my head, ensuring that I wouldn't get in his way as he punished my sensitive nipples and the even more delicate place between my legs.

He would strap one breast at a time, lashing that tiny hard bud until I cried out, tears dripping down my face as the terrible burn consumed me like fire. I whimpered and begged, but nothing stopped the eventual downfall of that belt on my tender chest.

At first, he just concentrated on my nipples. He didn't just stop there though. He used the end of the belt to spank the rest of my breasts. I could see the red marks rising on my pale skin and I continued to cry because it hurt so very much.

He took that belt between my legs once more.

"This little pussy is going to be just as red as your bottom by the time I'm through with you," he warned, and I keened with both fear and arousal.

I wanted to hate it. I wanted to hate him for his cruelty, for his harshness when he dealt with me, but I couldn't.

Not when my body was reacting like this. Pain and pleasure twisted together in a depraved inferno of sensation, leaving me breathless with arousal. Even as tears rolled down my cheeks, wetness seeped from my pussy and he could see every last glistening droplet of it on my thighs.

The belt whipped between my legs once more and my clit pulsed with need. My cries of pain morphed into something that sounded more like passionate moans for more.

He laid the belt just below my breasts and his punishing fingers delved in the place he had just so cruelly punished. They glided along my scalded flesh and I keened. Even the gentlest touch hurt, reigniting the fiery burn from the lash. Carefully, he spread my pussy open and revealed my hard and very needy clit to his view. He put me on display for him.

He lifted the belt once more.

"No. Please. I'm sorry. Please don't, sir," I pleaded.

Again, my pleas fell on deaf ears.

He whipped the belt three times. It fell directly onto my clit and I screamed, even as my pussy spasmed with arousal.

"You protest, little mate, but you're so much wetter now that this little pussy has been properly spanked," he said firmly.

I knew it was true. I was wetter and when he pressed two fingers directly inside my pussy, his advance was made easy by the sheer amount of arousal leaking down my thighs. He pumped those fingers in and out of me roughly and I moaned, lifting my hips for him.

Fuck.

I wanted him so badly.

His fingers cupped my scalded pussy and the feeling of his flesh on mine was as possessive as it was painful. His palm pressed directly against my clit, he gently moved it in a circular motion, and my body almost jolted in his hands.

"Oh, God. Please," I begged.

"This naughty little pussy hasn't earned the privilege of orgasm yet," he chided. Without hesitation, he started paddling my wet folds once more and I writhed and moaned from those punishing blows. My thighs flexed and splayed for him, even as he continued ensuring that I very truly felt put in my place by my mate.

His dominance was as thorough as it was punishing.

I knew I would think twice before I went off and did something against his wishes again.

He spread my folds once more and spanked my clit hard enough to make yelp and cry, leaving my already sore flesh stinging and aching.

. . .

WHEN HE WAS DONE, he ripped the vine holding my wrists captive with ease. He gripped my hands and pulled me up, before he deposited me on my knees in front of him. His cock jutted hard and erect in front of my face and I whimpered, even as my pussy clenched tightly with need.

"Open your mouth," he demanded.

I obeyed as an anxious shiver raced down my spine.

As soon as I opened my lips, he thrust his cock onto my tongue. He wasn't gentle and he didn't give me any time to get used to his size. I struggled to draw in a breath as he plunged into me and in his harshness, even more tears leaked from the corners of my eyes. He peered down at me and that only seemed to make him use my mouth even harder.

He liked seeing me cry. He liked making it hurt even more.

I didn't want to admit it, but I liked it too. I hated it at the same time.

"You will suck my cock, little mate, and then you're going to swallow every last drop. You're going to show me that you're very sorry by just how enthusiastically you worship my cock with that soft little mouth," he demanded, and I moaned around his length. His movements were rough, but I took every last thrust because that's what he wanted from me.

There was no kindness in the way he used me. He punished my throat with his cock and before I knew it, I was sore and aching there too. I opened my throat for him as much as I could, but his shaft was so long and his girth was so wide that I could only give so much. He took what he needed anyway.

I moaned and cried around his cock, my sounds utterly shameful. I gave my all into sucking his cock and when he finally groaned with his own pleasure, my pussy quivered with delight. My bottom, breasts, and pussy were so sore, and it made me wet just thinking about how much they hurt. How he had made them hurt.

I grew even wetter when I remembered the rest of the pack, that they were watching as my mate used my mouth as hard as he desired.

"I'm going to come in your mouth, little mate, and you're going to swallow everything I give you," he demanded. "Do you understand?"

"Yes, sir," I whined, speaking with his cock still in my mouth. The sound of my tongue bouncing off his shaft was embarrassingly shameful. My voice shook, gagged by the thickness of his cock and I shivered, feeling my own arousal gather between my thighs. I shivered with need as his length pulsed against my tongue.

I found myself wanting to please him. I craved everything he wanted to give me.

I realized at that moment that I was a dirty little girl.

I wanted these depraved things. I wanted him to touch me in the places I wasn't supposed to be touched. I needed every drop of his cum in my belly.

I sucked him more fervently than before. I showed him my devotion with my mouth, swirling my tongue around his length and suckling hard around his thick head. He groaned once again, and his thighs trembled just the slightest bit before his speed spurted deep into my throat. Desperately, I swallowed around him, taking every last drop into my belly just like he demanded of me.

My thighs clenched hard.

I grew even wetter than before.

My desire for orgasm intensified. I had just suckled him to completion, but I craved his enormous cock inside me. I wanted to come all over it.

His seed was warm and thick, spurting in thick gobs into my belly until he'd emptied completely. I took it all and when he was finished, he pulled free from my mouth. For a long moment, he stared down at me and I knelt there before him, feeling so incredibly small right there in front of him.

On my knees for my alpha. In my rightful place as the omega of the pack.

He reached for me and offered me a hand. I took it tentatively, unsure of what he would do to me next. He roughly pulled me to him and kissed me, his lips gentle and cruel in the same breath. While his lips ravaged mine, he reached between my legs and pinched my clit hard. I cried out and he swallowed my sounds, only punishing my clit even more harshly than before. I struggled in his arms to take it, but he was so strong, and I was so much smaller than he was. I whimpered and tried to submit to his cruelty, but it was so very hard.

"You will bend over that very same log you were spanked over and show yourself to me. Show me where you need to be fucked, my naughty mate," he commanded, and a whine escaped my throat. Even before he made me do it, his words made a flush of humiliation come over my face and a rush of liquid heat gather between my thighs.

His knowing eyes peered back at me as if he could see right through me. As if he already knew what he was doing to me.

My blood practically simmered with heat. The very air that drew into my lungs felt hot and my heart wanted to beat right out of my chest.

I needed to come, but most of all, I needed his cock.

Hesitantly, I obeyed his instructions. I bent over the fallen log, grateful for the thick coating of moss that padded underneath my belly. With trepidation, I arched my back and presented my swollen wet pussy for him. He kicked my heels a bit wider, putting me on display even more than before. I felt so terribly exposed like this, knowing he was staring straight at my nakedness and that he could see just how very wet that this was making me. Not only that, but everyone else could see it too.

I shivered when the thought of all those eyes on me crossed my mind.

"Spread yourself for me. Show me that naughty little bottom hole," he declared, and I shuddered with shame. When I didn't immediately obey his command, his palm smacked upward, spanking my pussy hard. I cried out and hurriedly gripped at my cheeks while he continued to punish my wet and very sensitive folds. When I could manage it, I spread myself wide for him and keened with humiliation as I showed him my virgin hole.

He finally stopped spanking my pussy then.

His cock nestled at my entrance and I breathed a sigh of relief that he wasn't going to take my bottom just yet. My pussy tightened with need and I hoped that he would allow me to come for him soon. I didn't know how much more I could take.

He was hard again. For me. That should have scared me, but I didn't know any better. Not yet.

I arched my back, pressing up against his thick length. His cockhead pushed against my pussy, stretching me slowly and I whimpered. He was so big, and my pussy felt so very tight. He'd fucked me before, but he was so enormous that it felt like the first time, every time.

His advance into me was gradual just to show me that he could. He claimed my body inch by gloriously long inch, all while I held myself open for him. In a possessive maneuver, he trailed his fingers up my thigh as he pressed even more deeply into my pussy until his thumb rested directly on top of my bottom hole.

I whimpered nervously. He pistoned his hips backwards, pulling his cock out leisurely until he slammed it back into me. I cried out at the sudden ache as he forced himself inside me and then back out. His thumb gathered my wetness and then he pushed inside my bottom with his thumb at the same time that he fucked my pussy.

I shuddered with a violent wave of desire and my pussy spasmed around his cock, gripping him tightly with my need.

I didn't want to come this way, but I had a feeling that I wasn't going to have a choice. His thumb fucked my bottom roughly while his cock claimed my pussy. There wasn't a single ounce of tenderness in the way he used me then. He fucked me so hard that it hurt. He punished me with his massive cock, and I took every last inch of it.

I screamed. I cried. I begged for mercy and I received none.

That only earned me a harder fucking. My inner walls fluttered around his length and I pleaded for him to forgive me.

Arousal blazed hot inside me as the pain from his punishment melded together with the pleasure coursing through my veins. My clit pulsed and my bottom tightened around his thumb, depraved desire pumping through me. There was nothing about being taken this way that wasn't shameful, from his finger inside my virgin ass to the pack watching him fuck me.

Naked. Wet. On display for everyone watching.

I was so turned on. I wanted to come. I needed it so very badly.

"Please let me come, alpha. Please let me come all over your cock," I begged. Every word that left my lips made me shudder with embarrassment, even as it made my pussy clench around his cock.

"Do you really want it, omega? Do you think you deserve to come?"

"Please, alpha," I pleaded. His hips slapped against my

pussy, the motion hard and just as punishing as his palm had been against my sensitive flesh.

My clit pulsed, throbbing with need.

"Answer me properly," he growled.

"Yes, sir," I whispered, my voice hoarse with my need.

"That's better," he replied calmly. "Brace yourself on the log, little mate. You do not have permission to come yet."

I whined with desperation. My cries sounded pitiful to my own ears, but it didn't matter.

My skin was feverishly hot. All I could think about was how good his cock felt in my pussy and how much his thumb in my bottom was turning me on. He used that digit to fuck my ass slowly and my tight little hole clenched around him. He chuckled knowingly before he thrust all the way forward, his cock bottoming out inside my pussy even more deeply than before.

"Good little girls get their pretty little pussies fucked, isn't that right, little mate?" he asked, and I trembled with arousal. I could feel my inner walls tightening around him, showing him exactly how much I needed him right now.

"Yes, sir," I whispered, arching my back as he dragged his cock in and out of me teasingly slowly.

"Bad little girls get fucked someplace else, don't they, little omega?"

I stilled as realization dawned on me.

"You were a bad little girl, weren't you?"

My mouth went dry and my heart felt like it was going to explode. His thumb pumped in and out of my bottom, as I slowly realized that I wasn't going to be able to come with his cock inside my pussy. He was going to make me come with his cock in my ass. He was going to punish me with that cock, the same way he'd already punished my throat.

"Please don't," I begged.

He removed his thumb and pressed two fingers roughly

inside of my asshole. He wasn't gentle because he was sending me a message. He was going to take my bottom with his cock whether I liked it or not.

"I was a bad little girl," I finally answered, the nervous anticipation in my voice making it tremble violently.

"Where are bad little girls fucked, my naughty little mate?"

His two fingers spread open and I cried out at the sudden painful stretch that blossomed across my asshole. His message was clear.

I was about to get my last virgin hole fucked for the very first time.

"You will answer me, little mate. Loud and clear so that the entire pack can hear," he demanded. I keened with shame and my entire body tightened around him. No matter what I did, I couldn't hide my desire like this, not with his cock pressed deep inside me, not when he could feel every time my pussy seized greedily around his cock.

No. I could hide nothing like this. My body was telling him exactly what I needed.

Flushed with my shame, I opened my lips and I said the words that he wanted to hear.

"Bad little girls are fucked in their bottom holes," I finally managed to say. A rush of wetness coated his cock and my nipples peaked against the moss-covered wood.

"Do you think I'm going to be gentle even though it's your very first time?" he asked, and my body shuddered hard.

"No, sir," I answered, my voice high-pitched and nervous.

"This wet little pussy is so very needy, isn't it?"

"Yes, alpha," I whispered, trying to hold myself together.

His other hand caressed my shoulder, trailing across until his fingers hugged my throat. His grip tightened, a maneuver of power that reminded me that I had never been in control.

Using his grasp on my throat as leverage, he pulled free

from my pussy and removed his fingers from my bottom, only to replace it with the head of his cock. He'd stretched me open only a little with those fingers and as he pressed forward with his thick girth, I realized how very much I was unprepared for what was about to happen.

His cock was so much larger. It stretched me wider and my body revolted, tightening around him in a panic. I lost control of myself then as a vicious burning pain raced up and down my spine, holding me captive as his punishing cock claimed my bottom for the first time. There was no gentleness in the way he took me. He knew it hurt. It was supposed to.

This was what would truly bring the punishment home. This was what would break me.

Here I was, naked and on display while my alpha took my ass in front of the entire pack. He'd told me he was going to fuck me like this, and he had been true to his word.

I hadn't known it could hurt this much. I wasn't prepared for how very much it turned me on either.

Even as my body shook with the painful ache of his advance, my pussy fluttered with need. My entrance was desperately empty, and my clit throbbed with sensation. The more his cock pushed into my bottom, the more I wanted to come.

I needed release badly.

With one final thrust, he pushed his entire length into my sore little asshole, and I keened as my body fought his intrusion. For a long moment, I struggled to take him and when his grip tightened just a bit around my throat, I found myself giving in and the pain started to fade just a little.

"Where is my cock, little omega?"

"In my bottom hole, alpha," I whispered, digging my nails into the wood beneath me. Waves of soreness still burst across my flesh and jolted straight down to my core, residual tremors of my body's reluctance to take him where he wasn't meant to be taken.

He thrust in and out of my bottom slowly, almost as if he was reminding me that he could. An indecent sounding moan escaped my lips and I clamped them together in shame, but then he started to use my bottom harder. Faster.

I moaned louder.

There was no kindness in the way he used my bottom. This was a punishment and it was meant to hurt, but what was even more shameful was the fact that I wanted to come this way. I liked it rough like this and the orgasm brewing deep inside me felt like a tidal wave that was hell bent on breaking me into pieces.

I knew that once it hit me that I would never be the same.

My pussy pulsed with need. My arousal dripped down my thighs and nipples hardened into tight little sensitive peaks that begged to be touched.

I needed to come, badly.

He needed to give me permission.

I began to beg. I didn't care how embarrassed it made me. I no longer thought about who would hear me or see me behaving like I was going into heat.

"You want to come, don't you? You want to come with my cock deep in your tight little bottom," he demanded, and my pussy squeezed with my desire.

He was right.

"I do. Please let me come, sir," I begged.

My face flushed, but my body demanded release. He'd taken me over his knee and spanked me with his hand. He'd whipped my ass with my own belt. He'd thrashed my nipples and my sensitive little pussy with it too. My throat was sore from his cock. My pussy was too, but even after all that and maybe especially because of it, I wanted to come. Badly.

I pleaded for the privilege. I promised to be a very good

girl if he would just let me orgasm. My words sounded desperate and needy and altogether pitifully shameful, but it didn't matter.

He owned me. I was his mate and he was my alpha. He decided when I would come and if he would even allow it at all.

Liquid arousal dripped down my thighs, direct evidence of how very much that thought turned me on. He'd taken every single ounce of control and claimed it for himself and now I waited for him, waited for permission to come as I trembled before him. He'd made me a wet little mess and I wanted him even more because of it.

He thrust in and out of my bottom hard.

"Come for me, little mate. You're going to come even harder than you ever have before and you're not going to stop until there are tears dripping down that pretty face. You're going to keep coming for me until you're sobbing and even then, I'm not sure I'm going to allow you to stop," he warned and the strangled sound of fear that left my throat revealed my terror.

He used my bottom hole hard. It hurt, but that only made me edge even closer to release. There was no fighting the orgasm that threatened to take me. It was going to destroy me once it hit. I knew that and there was nothing I could do to stop it.

My clit pulsed with sensation and I moaned as desire raced through me. My core quivered, quaking with need from the painfully pleasurable bottom fucking I was receiving. I shook with unreleased passion and my pussy tingled with arousal. Every second that passed amplified the needy bliss that was just out of reach.

At least, until it wasn't.

Agonizing ecstasy sliced through my core like a hot knife through butter. A strangled scream slipped through my lips and my pussy spasmed hard, tightening desperately around empty air as his cock speared in and out of my most reluctant hole. My clit pulsed and I moaned, drowning in the pleasurable bliss that his punishment had forced me to take.

"That's right, little mate. Come hard with my cock in your naughty little bottom," he murmured, and another orgasm broke over me with just as much intensity as the first.

I obeyed. I came so hard that I broke into a million little pieces. My thighs splayed and I writhed beneath him as he took my bottom as hard as he pleased. It was rough and my bottom ached, but I didn't care. It just made me come harder than ever.

I moaned and screamed with pleasure. I was so loud that I was sure that I was echoing through the forest. There was no doubt that the pack had heard me come. Kiba released my throat after that and shifted his fingers into my hair at the back of my scalp. He closed his fist and wrenched my head backwards, forcing me to face the betas who were watching me come so very shamefully.

My pussy clenched down hard. I didn't want to like it, but I did.

I screamed as another orgasm tore through me. My thighs shook and I was suddenly grateful for the support of the log beneath me. The back of my scalp burned as he pulled on my hair, tightening his fingers cruelly in order to remind me of my place.

He used me roughly, his thrusts punishing and forceful as he fucked me. Everything hurt. My pussy was sore, inside and out. My nipples throbbed from his fingers on my flesh. I could feel the painful ache from the belt all over my body.

I came harder because of it all. I lost total control and I drowned in pleasure. An endless black hole of desire consumed me.

My clit throbbed hard with bliss and my pussy clenched down tight. My passion cut through me so fiercely that I felt like I was being torn open from the inside out. Pain and pleasure twisted into one inseparable sensation. One orgasm bled into the next and soon I lost track of how many times I came for him.

It didn't matter anyway. I was going to come for him until he allowed me to stop. It didn't matter how sore I was or how much I begged him for mercy. It was up to him when this punishment ended.

With each subsequent orgasm, that became more and more clear.

The first few times I came for him, it felt wonderful and it had been exactly what I had needed. The more and more my releases ripped through me, the more painful they became until my breath hitched in my throat.

I lost control completely and I wailed as I came again.

Pain. Pleasure. Agony.

I no longer knew up from down. I couldn't form any coherent thoughts.

I was his and he was mine.

Ecstasy destroyed me from within, shattering me into a billion little shards of glass that would never be put back together again.

I started to cry.

And then he reached beneath my legs and pinched my clit hard.

I screamed as I broke.

He thrust in and out of my bottom far harder than before as he wrenched another orgasm from my overly sensitized body. He twisted my clit roughly, and I cried out.

I sobbed. Tears poured down my cheeks. My breath was ragged, and I struggled to draw in air, needy little pants of desperation echoing around me.

I begged for mercy. I pleaded to be allowed to stop coming for him.

My words didn't matter. He wasn't through with me.

I screamed. I cried. I sobbed for him as he forced me to orgasm again for him.

"Do you feel like you've been punished, my sweet little mate?" he asked.

I tried to answer but I couldn't. I wailed and nodded, trying to form words but I was no longer capable.

"One more orgasm, my little mate. One more and then it's all over," he said firmly, and I sobbed even harder knowing that it still wasn't done.

I obeyed because I had no other choice.

Sheer agony brutalized me from within as my body submitted to his command. Blazing fire scorched me as my core twisted in on itself in one last cruel orgasm that broke me so hard that I didn't know if I would ever stop crying. His seed spurted deep into my bottom and I screamed as wave after wave of harsh never-ending sensation slashed through me, over and over until I lost myself completely.

I don't know when he pulled his cock free from my bottom. I don't remember how I ended up in his lap with his arms around me. I just know his strength surrounded me and the tears continued to fall.

"I'm sorry. I'm so sorry," I whispered over and over again until he pressed his lips to my forehead and then my cheek until he kissed my lips, swallowing my cries once and for all.

"Shh. It's all over. You're forgiven, sweet mate," he whispered, and I curled into him, desperate for someone to hold onto. I clutched at his chest, knowing that person would always and forever be him.

CHAPTER 10

Dawn

I DON'T KNOW how long he held me for. It could have been minutes or hours, but it didn't matter. His soothing touch dried my tears. His calming fingers grazed up and down my naked back, quieting my cries and letting me know that everything was alright. His strong arms comforted me probably more than he would ever know. I sniffled and pressed my face into the curve of his throat, deeply breathing in his scent because it consoled me too.

"That's my good girl," he whispered, and my heart leapt in my chest.

He didn't ask me to speak and I was glad for it because I wasn't sure if I was even capable of forming words yet. Instead, he just allowed me to gather myself until I was ready to speak again.

"I love you," I finally whispered, and his arms tightened around me.

"I've loved you since the very first moment I laid eyes on you, sweet girl," he replied softly, and I lifted my eyes to meet his. They were full of love and adoration. He had meant every single word.

I felt so very light in that moment; he'd taken all my worries and stresses away from me. The only thing that mattered was the two of us. Right then, there was nothing else.

Just us and our destiny to become one.

I had fought it at first. I didn't want to accept his power over me, but as time went on, he claimed first my body, then my mind and ultimately, he'd conquered my heart.

Tentatively, I pressed my lips to his and kissed him. His palm cupped around the back of my head, taking control but only by a little. It was gentle and I breathed into him, reveling in that moment of perfection.

"What do we do now?" I asked, my voice shaking as I leaned back against him, trying to stop the trembling in my legs.

"Were you successful, little mate? Were you able to gather enough information about the scientific activities of the government?" he asked.

I turned back to him, surprised that he would even ask.

"You were punished for planning the break-in on your own and not telling me. You were also punished for disregarding my instructions to stay where I told you to stay. You were not punished for your idea itself, which was a good one. You've trained a long time to understand the different intricacies of scientific experimentation. Should the information you gathered prove fruitful, I'd like you to continue what you had planned. The only difference will be that you're going to do it by my side, rather than on your own. Do you understand me, Dawn?" he explained.

I dropped my eyes and nodded, feeling incredibly small and humbled before him.

"You're forgiven for all that. No more looking back at past regrets or mistakes. I want you to think about the future now. I want you to think about the sound of our children's laughter. I also want you to think about the pack and then I want you to think about the two of us, happy and safe. Now think about the fact that you helped make that all possible. I'm so very proud of you for that. You have a keen mind and I want you to always feel free to use it, but you must remember that I will forever be your alpha and you will always be my first and only love, my omega. My mate. You're mine, sweet girl. Never forget that," he continued and even though I was so very sore and sorry for what I had done, his words made me smile.

I opened my mouth hesitantly, before I swallowed back my nerves and answered his question.

"I took pictures of everything that I could," I said as I reached for my pants and slipped out the phone from my pocket. None of the guards had taken it and I had been relieved to still find it there several days later. I'd kept it turned off in order to preserve the battery. "Complete with the notes Ashe was able to obtain off the servers, I have more than enough information to replicate their work and take it for myself. I have a number of contacts in the pharmaceutical industry that would be more than ready to buy this kind of research and develop it into production. This work would forever change the human world, giving them access to longer life and the capability to overcome many issues of infertility."

"What would you need?" he asked.

"A lab. If we returned to the place where you first found me, I could finish conducting my research there in secret. They would stop looking for me once I completed what they wanted me to do and then once I finish, we could leave and take the pack somewhere safe," I suggested quietly, and he nodded.

"Then we will take you there," he replied.

* * *

It took days for my soreness and the marks from the belt on the backs of my thighs to fade, but I liked that. It reminded me of the day I declared my love for my alpha and it also made me think about his bold dominance over my body, mind, and soul. I would run my fingers along each one, using my nails to scrape the welts left behind and reliving the moments where he put me over his knees, whipped me with my own belt, and then took my ass for the very first time.

Every time I thought about it, it made me wet.

Kiba allowed me to wear the guard uniform as we traveled through the woods, but it didn't hide my arousal from him. He would smell when I was wet, and he'd pull me close and whisper in my ear that he was going to make me come for him until I screamed right before he stripped me naked. Sometimes he would take my pussy, other times my ass or my throat. One thing was always certain though. He would always leave me sore and satisfied.

I loved him for it. It was as though he knew what I needed before I knew it myself.

When we finally arrived back at the black site where the shifters had first found me, the pack stopped a distance away where it would be safe for them to hide for a while. Kiba escorted me closer to the building until I had to go the rest of the way alone.

Just as I was about to walk away, he grabbed my wrist and pulled me back to him, capturing me in a kiss that left me breathless and needy. His arms surrounded me, and his hands dipped down to cup my ass, squeezing into each cheek with such possessiveness that it made my pussy clench and liquid heat gather between my thighs.

"Make me proud, little mate," he whispered, his dark eyes searching mine.

"I will, alpha," I answered, and his resulting smile made my heart flutter in my chest.

"Good, because when you're finally through here, I'm going to breed you hard, my pretty little mate," he warned, and a delightful shiver raced down my spine.

The thought of bearing his children made me tremble with need.

"I haven't given you the pleasure of my knot yet, omega, but I will soon and when I do, I'm going to make sure I leave you very sore and spent. Think about that when you're in there carrying out your science. Think about my cock deep in your little pussy giving you exactly what you need and exactly what you deserve," he promised, and a soft cry escaped my lips.

With just his words, my legs went weak. By the darkening look in his eyes, he knew it too.

"Promise?" I challenged him softly, just to see his eyes narrow because it made my pussy clench even tighter with need.

"I promise, little mate," he growled.

I shuddered hard.

He turned me around and slapped my ass hard.

"Time to go now," he instructed, and I nodded.

I walked away from him and couldn't help myself as I turned back to face him. He smiled and I did too, but it was time to get to work.

When I strode inside this time, I entered through the front door that Amy had brought me into so very long ago, only this time it was on my terms and no one else's. I was quickly whisked away by security and not long after, Amy walked in. Her bun was just as tight as that first day when we'd sat across from each other on the plane.

My interrogation began as soon as she arrived. She questioned where I'd been for so long, what I'd been doing in the woods and who had taken me. I answered her questions truthfully for the most part, informing her that the shifters were instinctually programmed to come together to breed after a certain amount of time. I didn't tell her that an alpha had risen, nor did I tell her that he had taken me for his mate. I didn't tell her that every once in a while, he stripped me bare, forced me over his knees and spanked me. None of that was important, at least not to her anyway.

What was important was the future of my children and of my newfound family, my pack. I had to ensure their safety and their wellbeing.

"The shifters want their freedom, that's why they've been behaving more aggressively over the past several months. They've felt trapped and unable to carry out their basic instinct to breed, so that's made them both uneasy and more hostile than you've ever seen before," I explained, and she looked back at me with a certain amount of doubt.

"How do I know what you're saying is true? They killed people here and it's rumored on the upper levels that they attacked another government black site. How can I believe you when the shifters already have blood on their hands?" she pressed.

"They took me captive as collateral. I was their bargaining chip, should they need one, until every last shifter was freed from government captivity. They've gotten what they wanted. There will be no more attacks or bloodshed. Hold off on any further confrontations and you'll see no more aggression from them," I continued.

Her nails drummed on the table, clicking loudly in the silence between us.

She studied me intently, but I gave away nothing. Everything that befell us now was dependent on the success of this conversation. The pack and I would never be safe if the government continued searching for us. To be truly honest though, the humans would only be hurting themselves if they went after the shifters.

The wolves were powerful, practically immortal and weak to only one thing. They were the stronger predator and were far above humans on the food chain.

If they came after us, more of them were going to die.

Many of them.

And this time, I'd protect what was mine.

My future. My pack. My children.

I'd protect my alpha.

Amy cleared her throat, carefully considering what she was going to say next.

"If what you say is true, then we should reevaluate our strategy of how we deal with the shifter population. But as I understand, aren't the majority of them infertile? How could they come together to breed then?"

I licked my lips as I thought about how I would respond.

"As a biologist, I've been taught to question everything. I've always thought that there is a rational explanation behind every unexplained phenomenon; we just haven't discovered the true cause behind it yet. This feels different though. The wolf shifters feel intricately tied to nature, almost in a magical way. Maybe it's the timing of the lunar cycle. Maybe it's the coming red moon that's reawakened their birth cycle for the first time in hundreds of years. I'm not sure of what it is, but I've seen them in their natural environment. I've seen that magic and I believe it to be true," I finally replied.

"Perhaps it is as you say and it's possible that we just haven't figured out the scientific explanation yet," she said carefully, although there was an air of disbelief in her tone.

"Maybe. Maybe not. Either way, perhaps it's better to let them be. There hasn't been a record of this kind of occurrence ever. I could continue to study them for your department and possibly, I could come up with a scientific explanation of how their infertility has been seemingly reversed," I offered.

Her expression turned to me with interest.

"You would continue your work for us, even after everything you've been through?" she asked with a raised eyebrow.

"I would, but I want access to everything. I also would like clearance to come and go as I please. I don't want to remain trapped underground. I need to feel the sun," I demanded. I remained strong, kept my voice steady and calm. Lifting my chin just the slightest bit, I sat back in my chair, keeping my spine straight and sure and as confident as I could manage.

I was a very strong woman and even though I was alone right now, I had the power of my alpha and the pack behind me.

That made me feel invincible.

And it showed.

Amy cowed just slightly in front of me, her chin dropping and her shoulders rounding a little bit. It gave her away. I knew even before she answered that I had already won.

"I don't think that's too much to ask for," she replied a bit more softly.

"Good. I'd like to return to the lab now. I've got several notes and ideas I'd like to jot down as well as a multitude of samples to catalog and analyze," I said expectantly. "First though, I'd love to take a shower and change out of these clothes."

"I bet you do," she beamed. "Dr. Livingston will be relieved to hear you're back and that you're safe."

"I'm looking forward to seeing him too," I smiled.

"We're glad to have you back, Dr. Lowe," she said, reaching out to shake my hand.

"I'm happy to be too," I replied.

She opened the door for me, and I strode out, descending into the black site building on my own. I returned to the small apartment that had been prepared for me and stripped naked as soon as I shut the door behind me, leaving the dirty guard uniform on the floor. I took the longest and hottest shower of my life, scrubbing off the filth of the forest as thoroughly as I could. I dug my fingers into my scalp and massaged in first shampoo and then conditioner until I felt fully clean.

I ran my fingers along my body. I felt harder, my muscles firmer, and when I looked in the mirror, I noticed that I was more toned than I was several weeks ago.

When I was finally finished showering, I ordered a big meal. I chose a burger and fries with more toppings than I could count. While I was waiting for them to bring it to me, I powered on the laptop on the desk.

I checked the date. It had been over a month since I'd last been here. I hadn't realized so much time had passed. A month ago, I led a lonely life, worrying about the next grant deadline and the revisions that were due on my student's manuscript. Now I had a family and a mission.

That night, I got started.

* * *

THE WEEKS PASSED QUICKLY as I threw myself into my research. I worked on multiple things at once, from experiments confirming the infertility research and a number of tests looking into the validity of the immortality project. In secret, I kept records of what I was to eventually sell to the pharmaceutical industry, ensuring the notes I kept were hidden in a notebook I only took out when there was no one else around.

I knew there were cameras watching the lab, so I kept the notebook in my bedroom. I'd searched the room up and down and found nothing indicating that I was being watched there, so I kept it on the top shelf of my closet with the clothes that they had provided me with.

I snuck out some nights to be with Kiba, using the excuse that I needed some air under the stars. No one was particularly worried about my activities though, and I was never questioned. Knowing I was approaching the end of my work, Kiba and I planned our next moves together, including the one where I would approach my connections in industry.

We were going to ensure a bidding war between companies, maximizing our profits once everything came to a head.

He also made sure to send me back to the lab very sore and very satisfied, time and time again. Oftentimes, I was left wearing his mark, whether it was his seed drying on my thighs or the welts of a switch on my backside.

It made me remember that my place was with him.

I pretended to be the good little scientist and when I was sure of my work on the beta infertility problem, I presented it to the department. With my project nearly complete, I began to make preparations to leave.

Thus far, Amy had made no moves to go after the pack. Everything stayed quiet and as more time passed, the more confident I became that we'd be able to live free without worry of the government's need to be involved.

In secret, I backed up all of my data to a hard drive that Ashe had provided me and when I was ready, I slipped it out to Kiba in the dead of night.

Soon after that, my clearance was withdrawn, and Amy flew me back home. My work was done with the Department of Paranormal Activity. I signed a number of nondisclosure agreements ensuring that I wouldn't speak of the knowledge I gained under their employment. In order to keep up appearances, I once again assumed my position as faculty at the University of Connecticut and continued life as usual.

Only it wasn't.

I met in secret with top executives around the world. I presented the data I'd accumulated and set the terms to my liking. I would provide them with the formulas and findings only in the event that I remain anonymous and that I would have nothing to do with the future of any of the research they might perform. I did this in order to protect myself and the rest of the pack.

Kiba and the betas integrated into normal society as they had done for centuries, hiding in plain sight and keeping me safe from afar. Kiba himself resided in my home, ensuring that I was never too far from him or his cock.

He still hadn't given me his knot though. I didn't quite understand what that meant. When I asked, he simply told me that it would hurt, but I would enjoy it nonetheless. I was scared of what it would entail, but I knew better than to question him any further.

He told me he would breed me when the time was right.

The weeks passed as I negotiated a bidding war. Sometimes I would bring Kiba with me to some of the meetings and other times I went alone. By the time it was all over though, I was more than pleased with the resulting outcome.

Along with the purchase of a massive plot of more than one thousand square miles of uninhibited forests in Canada, I was paid more than five billion dollars combined with a ten percent royalty of product sales that would continue on indefinitely, passing along to my children and their children's children. This would afford my pack what they needed for a long time to come. This would give them the kind of freedom they never had before. No longer would they need to live separate lives scattered all over the world. They could be together as a pack.

Once the papers were signed and the funds were deposited in an account opened under a false name that Ashe created for all of us, we slipped away to our new home.

Together, we made a small community on the fringes of the world, safe in a place where we could all be together and where Kiba and I could sire as many children as possible.

When Kiba and I were finally settled in our own log cabin in the middle of the forest, safe from prying eyes and dangerous enemies, he pulled me into his arms and whispered the words in my ear that I so desperately wanted to hear.

"It's time for you to be bred, little omega."

CHAPTER 11

Dawn

I SHIVERED HARD in his arms, waiting for what might come next. We were safe from the outside world now and that meant I could carry his children without fear that either they or I would come to any harm. Our little corner of North America was practically impossible to get to except by air, and even then, the places to land a plane were few and far between, which afforded us a great deal of safety.

It also meant that we would remain uninterrupted.

That no matter how loud I screamed, we wouldn't be disturbed. No one else was coming and the pack wouldn't dare to intervene.

Kiba liked it that way and even though I didn't want to admit it, I liked it too.

His arms tightened around my waist, reminding me what was to come.

"Are you afraid, my little mate?" he asked, and a strangled

sound of need and fear escaped my throat. It was true I was afraid, but there was a deep part of my soul that needed this, that craved to be taken like this.

"Yes, alpha," I finally managed to whisper.

Even now, I was ready for him. My pussy had tightened hard at his pronouncement that I was going to get fucked good and hard, that he was going to breed me at last. I didn't know what that meant, nor did I care because I knew I was safe in Kiba's hands. I trusted him with my life.

He kissed the top of my head, then my cheek, and eventually he lightly bit at my throat. I trembled, pressing my thighs together with anxious curiosity. I could feel myself growing wet knowing that soon I would be beneath him with his cock speared deep between my legs.

"You've been working so hard for so very long, my sweet mate, but I think it is about time that I remind you that I'm in control, isn't it?" he whispered, and I practically quivered in his arms. My legs felt weak, and I used his strength to keep myself upright.

My clit pulsed with need.

"Do you need me to remind you of your place, omega?"

"Yes, alpha," I murmured, my voice shaking with nervousness.

"You're wearing far too many clothes for a reminder like that, aren't you, little mate?"

I whimpered quietly in response.

Without a word, he turned me toward him so that I faced him. Methodically, he grasped the zipper of my gray pullover and slid it down, pressing the fabric open to reveal the clothes underneath it. Then he pushed it off my shoulders, letting it fall to the floor in a crumpled heap. I didn't move to pick it up. Next, he removed my long-sleeved t-shirt by slowly pulling it over my head and after that, he unbuttoned my jeans and pushed them down over my hips. He lifted each foot and removed my boots and socks, leaving me in just a matching pink bra and panty set that he'd purchased for me to wear for him.

The fire in the fireplace beside us crackled strong, keeping me warm despite the fact that he had stripped me of my clothing.

"Remove your bra and panties. Slowly. Sexily. Show your pretty little body off to your alpha," he instructed, and I panted with heat. A feeling stronger than need came over me, a sort of primal if not magical instinct to mate. My skin tingled with a mystical energy and when I lifted my hands in front of my face, my skin almost seemed to sparkle.

Maybe it was magic. Maybe it was fate.

"Destiny," Kiba breathed. "We are meant to be one. The earth calls for this."

It felt right.

I carefully reached behind my back and undid the clasps of my bra one by one. The delicate lingerie popped open from the back and I hesitantly rounded my shoulders forward, allowing the straps to slip down my arms. Carefully though, I held the cups in place with my fingers. I didn't bare myself just yet.

Instead, I swayed my hips from side to side. Kiba growled low in appreciation and my core squeezed tight. I moaned softly, feeling the seat of my panties grow even wetter against my skin. When I was ready, I allowed the bra to drop to the floor, revealing my breasts to his view. My nipples were already pebbled into tight little buds, just begging for his fingers to pinch them and for his lips to suckle them, maybe even for his teeth to bite them.

Perhaps he'd do all of the above.

I fingered the edge of my panties next, just slipping my fingertips beneath the hem and gliding them along my flesh. It seemed as though my nipples peaked even harder than before, aching for him to take me hard just like I needed, just like what I wanted.

My skin blazed with scalding heat as I carefully slid my panties down my hips, inch by inch until I paused, right before I completely bared my pussy to him. Instead, I slipped my fingers in between my thighs, just touching the soaking wetness that was dripping down my folds. I just glanced against my sensitive clit and gasped at the incredible sensation that jolted through me at that simple touch.

"Naughty girl, touching yourself without permission. It appears I'm going to have to start reminding you of your place with that naked bottom over my knee, isn't that right, little mate?" he whispered, and I whimpered with arousal.

My hand stilled and for a moment, I contemplated removing my fingers, but I wanted more than just that touch. I wanted to come. Through hooded eyes, I gazed up at him and boldly decided to continue even though he was watching. He smiled and his eyes darkened, suddenly reminding me of a feral beast about to strike.

And he was coming for me.

"Keep it up, little mate, and that bare little bottom isn't the only thing that's going to get spanked tonight," he warned, and a visible shudder racked my small frame. I bit my lip. Was I brave enough to continue? Could I handle his punishing palm?

Did I want to? What if I did?

I wanted to be thoroughly reminded of my place. I wanted to forget everything that happened in the past and I wanted to only think about the future.

About us. About the child he was going to put in my belly tonight.

Nothing else.

He stalked toward me and I backed up into the wall. His large frame surrounded me, making me feel smaller and more vulnerable than ever. One hand slapped against the wall next to my head and the other knocked my hand out of the way, only to grasp my panties in his thick fingers instead.

"I'm going to very much enjoy turning that bare little ass of yours and that pretty pink pussy red with my palm, naughty mate."

"I'm not afraid," I countered, even though I knew it was a lie.

"You should be," he answered darkly and my pussy clenched hard in response. He pulled at my panties just a little, dragging the lace across my clit, back and forth. Waves of desire compounded through me, swirling and intensifying with every last stroke. I moaned and shuddered with need, arching my hips against him and silently begging for more.

"Are you enjoying this?" he asked, and I should have heeded the warning in his tone, but I didn't. I was too far gone to recognize how his body had stiffened or the simmer of a threat that was hidden behind his words.

"Yes, sir," I murmured as I edged my own fingers along his strong forearms.

He chuckled, amused at my reaction. Then he stopped rubbing my clit with the lace of my panties. I whined at the loss of sensation, wanting more than he'd given me.

"What do you need, little mate?"

"To be reminded of my place, sir," I replied.

"That's exactly what's going to happen. Are you ready?" he asked.

"Yes, sir," I whimpered, feeling my arousal catapult inside me, looking for an out.

"Good."

His grip on my panties tightened and then he roughly ripped them from my body. The fabric pinched hard at my sensitive lips and fiery agony burned across my wet folds. I pitched forward, but his body was there to block me, forcing me to quiver through every last wave of painful sensation that washed over me.

"Did that hurt, little mate?"

"It did, sir," I whimpered.

"It was supposed to. And I promise you this, that little pussy is going to be a whole lot sorer by the time I'm finally through with you, omega," he said firmly.

My legs trembled and practically gave out beneath me. The need to flee quivered through me for a long second before I pushed it away. I had feared him before but now I did more than ever and by the look in his eyes, he knew it too.

His fingers just traced along my aching flesh, lightly touching where the panties had pinched me. I panted with need and when he parted my folds and stroked my clit, I hoped that he would allow me to come.

Without warning, he pinched my sensitive bud hard enough to make me cry out.

"No, not yet sweet mate. You're not going to be allowed to come for a good long while and if you do, you will walk out of this cabin and bring me three switches like you did on the very first day we met. Then I will walk you to the town center, completely naked where I will bind you and switch that bare little body until you're sobbing. If you were a bad little girl in taking that punishment, I'd make you take my cock right there in front of the entire pack. If you're a very good girl though and took it well, I would allow you to crawl back here on your knees, where you would beg me for the privilege to come all over my knot," he growled.

Liquid heat rush between my bare thighs, straight onto his fingers. My entire body tightened, and I heatedly wondered if he could feel the effect he was having on me.

"I won't come, sir," I pleaded.

"Good girl," he replied darkly, his eyes sparkling.

He was enjoying this. He liked keeping me wet and needy and afraid.

I'd never admit it, but I liked it too. A lot.

His fingertips left my pussy and traveled up to caress my nipples. His touch was gentle at first. He surrounded them, softly tweaking them until they were stiff and aching with need. After that though, his touch hardened, pinching my nipples more aggressively until I cried out with pain. He took them and stretched them out toward him, before twisting them harshly. I whimpered and then he released one. I gasped with relief until his thick fingers slapped at the breast still in his grasp.

When he did it again, the slap was firmer, the sting more intense. He continued to spank my breast, keeping a tight hold on my nipple and ensuring that each spank met its mark. Every last one hurt and he made sure they did, until the entirety of my left breast was pink from his punishing hand. When he was satisfied, he slapped my breast hard enough to pop my nipple free from his fingers. A volley of pain splintered from my tender bud as the blood rushed back to it, but I took it all because that's what he wanted. I whimpered as he took my right one into his fingers next.

He repeated this punishment and even though I knew what to expect, it was somehow worse because of it. I squirmed and begged as he slapped my breasts, but every strike met its mark. He took his time and made sure to leave me sore and aching, before he spanked my breast hard enough to free it from his hold once more.

My breasts throbbed. He grasped my shoulders and spun me around, forcing me to press my naked back against his chest. One arm wound around my waist. His free hand settled over my nipple and I stiffened.

He spanked it. Hard.

The pain that blossomed over my aching buds was sharp

like a knife. He slapped the other one with the flats of his fingers, not listening to the whimpers and pleas that fell from my lips. He punished my nipples thoroughly until my cries became more desperate.

I had no doubt that he could make me cry simply from this alone.

When he finally stopped, I whimpered and tried to catch my breath. Those punishing fingers descended between my thighs, gliding along my sensitive folds and finding my shameful secret.

I was soaked, absolutely positively soaking wet, and I knew it.

Now he'd discovered it too.

"It seems that despite your protests, you enjoyed having your pretty breasts spanked, didn't you, sweet mate," he murmured.

His finger stroked up and down my clit.

"Yes, alpha," I shuddered, feeling my inner walls flutter with arousal.

Quickly, he slapped my pussy and I cried out at the unexpected sting.

"Don't worry. That needy little pussy is going to be so much wetter before I'm through with you," he promised darkly, and my heart beat heavy in my chest.

I wanted to find out more. I wanted to know how far I could go. I wanted to know what I could take and what he wanted to give.

I decided to push him.

"Promises, promises," I taunted.

"Such a brave little omega you are, aren't you? We'll see if you're still just as brave after you're sobbing over my knee with that bare little bottom and that wet little pussy both very thoroughly spanked," he countered.

I stood before him afraid and wet and unbelievably

aroused. He stared down at me with those icy blue eyes and I watched them darken with undeniable threat. I'd pushed him and he knew it. Now he was going to have to take me in hand.

My pussy clenched, knowing that what was to come would hurt.

I shivered hard and rolled my upper lip at him, daring him, challenging him as my alpha. He rose to the task, just like I had known he would. He grasped me around the waist and sat down on the bed behind him, tossing me over his knees with little to no effort at all.

He used one ankle to spread my legs wide, revealing my bare and very wet pussy to him. He wanted to expose me, and a shiver of shame raced through me. My lips opened just a bit as I struggled to draw in air. Being forced into this position made me so hot and it made my very core quiver with desire of the unknown.

"Lift that pretty bottom for me. Show me where you need to be punished," he instructed, and I whimpered quietly as I obeyed. He groaned in appreciation and swept his palm over my bared backside. When I splayed my thighs even wider, he growled, and a rush of arousal gathered between my thighs.

I loved when he looked at me like this. It made my pussy burn with desire and the rest of me positively quiver with it.

The air caressed at my very wet and naked skin, reminding me of just how exposed I was. He grasped my bottom cheeks then and spread me wide, looking at every square inch of my bare flesh just because he could. I could feel myself tense and the realization that he could see me tighten in the most shameful way crossed my mind. I whimpered softly as he ran a single finger over my bottom hole, another reminder that he would do as he pleased regardless of what I did or said.

That made me hot. Needy.

I was so very aroused.

"Please," I pleaded, hoping he would touch me. I wasn't quite sure what I was begging for. Did I want him to spank me? Did I want to hurt for him?

Maybe I did.

I didn't have to wait long.

He released my bottom and used the flat of his palm to spank the lower curves of my ass, ensuring to catch the upper portion of my thighs. He didn't give me any time to get used to his harshness. The spanking started hard and fast. Why did this make my pussy quiver with need? Why did I have to push him so that he could punish me? Conquer me?

Why did I need him to remind me of my place like this?

I cried out as he spanked me, the pain quick and ruthless to render me into a trembling punished little mess. I tried to hold my bottom up for him, but it was useless. Each time his palm cracked against my flesh, I felt myself tense and try to squirm away. He wouldn't let me. He held me tight against him and that's when I felt him.

He was hard. His entire length pressed into my side, reminding me that even as he punished me, he was enjoying it. He liked reminding me that he was in charge and that he would always and forever be in control. He loved knowing that he could turn my pussy into a weeping puddle of arousal every time he turned me over his knee.

I liked it too. That's why I'd pushed him.

My pussy quivered with need, hot and ready to be taken hard by his cock. My bottom burned from his palm, but I knew my ordeal was far from over. He had yet to really punish my thighs and then there was the matter of my needy pussy.

I knew I was going to get spanked in both places before I was given permission to come. I knew I was going to be crying for mercy long before I would be allowed to have his cock where I needed it the most.

He would pause my spanking to lightly tease my clit with a single finger, taunting me with the pleasure he wouldn't yet give me. Over and over he did that until I was on the very edge of orgasm, only to pull away and leave me wanting.

He did it so much that I wanted to scream.

He spanked my bared backside hard and after that, he began to really punish my thighs. All throughout the spanking of my bottom, I'd been able to hold it together. It had hurt, but I'd been able to maintain control of myself.

My cries became more desperate. They were higher pitched, revealing just how much it hurt when he went after the backs of my legs like this. That only made him spank them harder.

I tried to stop it, but my breath hitched in the back of my throat. My eyes watered at a particularly hard stroke and I squeezed them shut. I blinked several times in order to keep my tears at bay. For a while, it worked.

"Spread your legs. It's time for your little pussy to get what it deserves," he instructed, and I whimpered as I splayed my legs open for him. I knew it was going to hurt, but I also knew it would hurt more if I didn't show obedience.

"That's a good girl," he murmured.

Carefully, he laid his fingers against my wet folds and then slid them back and forth, gliding along my wetness.

"You're so very wet, my omega," he observed, and I shuddered with my arousal, naked over his knee. I closed my eyes, even though that did nothing to hide my true feelings. He could see it all and he could see exactly how much he was affecting me right now.

He was going to spank my pussy.

He wasn't going to be gentle.

He was going to make it hurt and what terrified me was that I wanted it to.

It also turned me on.

The first crack of his fingers against my wet folds was like sheer agony. I screamed in surprise at his harshness, before I got a hold of myself. He swatted between my legs with fervor and before I knew it, the tears that had threatened to fall returned. He spanked my pussy hard and fast and soon my breath caught in my throat.

I whimpered and begged, but he didn't slow down. If anything, the spanks increased in intensity. He didn't allow me to squirm away from them or close my thighs to block his volley against my bared skin. He didn't allow me anything.

He was in control and he was going to make me cry.

His cock pulsed against my side. He felt enormous and I yearned to feel him deep between my thighs. I was so hot, so ready and so incredibly needy.

He spanked my poor scalded pussy even harder. Each spank was merciless, cruel and brutally harsh, which was exactly what I needed. I craved his punishment and with everything in me, I begged to be put in my place.

He forced my legs even wider and centered each spank on my clit then.

I couldn't hold back any longer. I started to cry and still the spanking didn't stop. He didn't let up and then something switched inside me. That's when the omega inside me truly awakened to my alpha.

It hurt so very much, but at the same time, desire for more came alive inside me. A mystical energy powered by my pleasure and my pain and the magical forces between us made me cry out from the intensity of emotions swirling around inside me.

In that moment, there was nothing more than him and

me. I was naked and exposed, getting punished over my mate's knee and it was so very perfect. My nipples ached. My bottom felt scalded and my pussy burned. He'd spanked every sensitive place on my body until I cried and because of that, my need was stronger than ever.

"Please," I begged. "Please fuck me."

"Do you think you deserve my cock now, little mate?"

"I need you," I pleaded. "Please give me your cock."

With a vicious growl, he threw me on my back on the bed. With ruthless strength, he tore his clothes right off and mounted me, pressing his massively hard erection against my bare wet little pussy.

"Do you want this, little mate? Do you really want your alpha's cock?"

"Yes. Please, alpha," I whimpered, spreading my thighs as wide as I could for him. His thumb traced the lines of tears down my cheeks and his cock throbbed hot against me.

"I like it when you cry for me, omega," he observed.

I whined, rocking my hips back and forth and dragging my sensitive clit up and down his iron length.

"I'm going to fuck you so hard and for so long that you'll cry again for me before the night is through," he promised, and I cried out.

"Please!"

He didn't make me wait much longer.

His cock speared into me with one single hard motion. He forced his entire length inside me without mercy, making my body take him all at once. I screamed as my body rebelled and tried to push him out. It was no use. He was big and hard, and he was going to take my pussy however he liked. My inner walls fluttered around him, stretched so very wide around his thick girth and I cried as my core constricted tight in a delicious agony that threatened to consume me.

"Oh, please. It hurts," I begged, and he began to move.

He thrust in and out of me so hard that his pelvis slapped against my wet folds, reminding me of just how hard he'd spanked my poor flesh just moments before. My punished backside pressed into the sheets, scalded and aching from his harsh punishing hand.

My nipples were sore too, but that didn't matter. He reached for them, tweaking them softly before he gripped them in a tight hold with his fingertips. I cried out, pain blossoming across my breasts as his cock ravaged my tight pussy. I was so wet that his advance in and out of me sounded so very loud and shameful.

It made me even hotter.

I wanted to come so much harder.

"Please. Let me come for you, alpha," I begged.

His lips devoured mine, capturing my pleas and swallowing them whole.

I gave into him completely, reveling in the feeling of his cock pressing in and out of me. I didn't care that it hurt because at the same time, it also felt so unbelievably good. My inner walls gripped at his shaft with a greed that I didn't know I was capable of. My skin burned with fever. All the sensitive places on my body ached with desire.

I wanted to come so very badly.

His cock speared into me and I felt myself quickly spiraling out of control. If he didn't give me permission to come soon, I didn't know if I would be able to stop it.

"Please. I can't," I pleaded. "It's too much."

"You will wait for my word, omega, or do you need another reminder of what happens to naughty little mates?" he threatened.

My pussy nearly spasmed around his cock.

My resulting cries were pitiful and desperate, so full of need that the very sound shamed me to the core. Not only that, but they made me even hotter knowing that he could hear every last one. He knew the effect he was having on me.

He knew he'd made me lose control. He also knew that he'd taken it for himself.

Slowly, he reached between my thighs and pressed his thumb against my clit. He just held it there, reminding me that if I orgasmed without permission, he was going to make me pay the price.

I begged. I pleaded. I whimpered and cried for him.

"Such a good, needy, wet little omega. You want to come very badly, don't you?"

"Yes, please. Please!"

"Do you feel in control now, my sweet mate?"

"No, sir," I whispered.

"Has your alpha reminded you of your place?"

"Yes, sir," I whimpered. "Please, sir. Please let me come for you."

My voice trembled with desperation. I feared my pleas would go unanswered. He could make me shake here with primal need for however long he wished. He could punish me by not allowing me to orgasm at all or he could put me in my place by edging me over and over until I was sobbing for relief.

I no longer knew what I was saying. I just begged. I told him I would be a good little mate, that I would be obedient, that I would give him whatever he wanted if he would just allow me the privilege of orgasm.

He gripped my throat with his hand, squeezing just tight enough to remind me that he held both my life and my pleasure in his hands.

"Come for me, omega. Come hard because your alpha demands it," he commanded.

I obeyed.

I came so hard I saw stars. My entire body clamped down

completely, feeling his cock so very deep inside me. I could feel my pussy tighten around him, milking his length for all it was worth. His fingers closed around my throat and I panted, drawing in the little amount of air that he allowed me. I wailed with the pleasure that coursed through me and I screamed from the residual ache of being reminded of his power over me, of the undeniable hierarchy between us.

My orgasm tore through my body with the viciousness of a knife. It ripped into me with such powerful sensation that I was left helpless against it.

It felt like my release lasted forever and I soon began to fear that it would never end. My clit throbbed hard under his thumb and I keened when I realized what would happen next.

He was going to make me come again. He was going to make me come until I was sobbing, all while his cock was fucking my tight little pussy. I thrashed beneath him. I pleaded for mercy, but none of it mattered.

That's what he wanted, and I didn't have any say.

I no longer had a choice.

Knowing that made me lose myself entirely.

I drowned in ecstasy. I reveled in it. I moaned and screamed and writhed for him, splaying my thighs and tensing my entire body as I came for him over and over again because that's what he wanted. I was helpless and vulnerable against the endless onslaught of pleasure that he gave me.

I came a second time and then a third. After that, I lost count of how many orgasms tore through me. I couldn't have kept track if I tried.

I was too far gone.

He'd taken me and ripped me open from the inside out, decimating my body, mind, and soul with overwhelming bliss. Pleasure and pain were one and the same. I didn't even attempt to tell one from the other.

He slammed his cock all the way inside me and then something changed.

The base of his shaft began to swell inside me, growing larger and larger as it stretched my pussy open from within. I screamed as I came all around him and my body took it all even though every muscle in me fought against him.

Agony.

Pleasure.

Darkness.

Light.

"That's it, omega. Take my knot. Take it all," he whispered, his own voice hoarse with arousal.

His words were my undoing.

I came again. I came so hard it broke me.

He'd conquered me once and for all with his cock. He mastered me completely and there was no more fight in me left to give. I was only vaguely aware of the fact that tears were dripping down my face, that sobs were racking my pleasure-ridden body. I cried for him as he stared down at me, all while his knot locked his cock into place inside me. His thumb circled on my clit, making me quake with passionate need and forcing me into yet another endless chasm of pleasurable bliss. I broke all around him, shattering into a million little pieces all over his cock.

He groaned and my core tightened hard, forcing me into yet another orgasm that was even more powerful than all the rest. I keened, screaming as I came. My entire body shook as agonizing ecstasy tore into me and then I felt him throb inside me. He was going to come.

I wanted it. I wanted him to give me every last drop.

I wanted him to breed me and he did.

I felt his seed spurt into me, one scalding volley after another that pelted so very deep inside me. His knot widened even further, ensuring that every last drop of his cum stayed inside me.

Magic surrounded us. The very air around us crackled with energy. I screamed and he growled low. Thunder roared and lightning flashed.

At that very moment, a spark of life hummed deep inside my core.

My baby.

He'd put a child inside me, and overwhelming joy consumed me. I cried with happiness. I sobbed with pleasure and I wept with hope for the future.

Kiba had given me everything.

Fate had brought us together and destiny had made us one.

He kissed me, his lips brutal and possessive and when he finally pulled away, his eyes were warm.

"I love you, my sweet mate. Forever and for always," he whispered.

"I love you too," I whispered back.

I curled in tight to his body, his knot still safely locked inside me. I closed my eyes and dreamed about what the future might hold, the laughter of my children, the joyful smiles of the pack, but most of all, I thought about the endless nights that Kiba and I would share together. I dreamed of it all and I didn't let it go, not even for a moment.

We would be together for the rest of our lives.

As alpha and omega.

As husband and wife.

And as mates that were forever fated to be one.

The End

Do you want to read a FREE book?

Sign up for Sara Fields' newsletter and get a FREE copy of Sold to the Enemy!

https://www.sarafieldsromance.com/newsletter

About Sara Fields

Sara Fields is a USA Today bestselling author that enjoys writing dark filthy fantasies with a whole lot of heart.

Website: https://www.sarafieldsromance.com/

Email: otkdesire@gmail.com

facebook.com/SaraFieldsRomance
twitter.com/Mrs_Sara_Fields
instagram.com/sarafieldsromance

Stormy Night Publications would like to thank you for your interest in our books.

If you liked this book (or even if you didn't), we would really appreciate you leaving a review on the site where you purchased it. Reviews provide useful feedback for us and our authors, and this feedback (both positive comments and constructive criticism) allows us to work even harder to make sure we provide the content our customers want to read.

If you would like to check out more books from Stormy Night Publications, if you want to learn more about our company, or if you would like to join our mailing list, please visit our website at:

http://www.stormynightpublications.com

MORE STORMY NIGHT BOOKS BY SARA FIELDS

Claimed by the General

When Ayala intervenes to protect a fellow slave-girl from a cruel man's unwanted attentions, she catches the eye of the powerful general Lord Eiotan. Impressed with both her boldness and her beauty, the handsome warrior takes Ayala into his home and makes her his personal servant.

Though Eiotan promises that Ayala will be treated well, he makes it clear that he expects his orders to be followed and he warns her that any disobedience will be sternly punished. Lord Eiotan is a man of his word, and when Ayala misbehaves she quickly finds herself over his knee for a long, hard spanking on her bare bottom. Being punished in such a humiliating manner leaves her blushing, but it is her body's response to his chastisement which truly shames her.

Ayala does her best to ignore the intense desire his firm-handed dominance kindles within her, but when her new master takes her in his arms she cannot help longing for him to claim her, and when he makes her his own at last, his masterful lovemaking introduces her to heights of pleasure she never thought possible.

But as news of the arrival of an invader from across the sea reaches the city and a ruthless conqueror sets his eyes on Ayala, her entire world is thrown into turmoil. Will she be torn from Lord Eiotan's loving arms, or will the general do whatever it takes to keep her as his own?

A Gift for the King

For an ordinary twenty-two-year-old college student like Lana, the idea of being kidnapped from Earth by aliens would have sounded absurd… until the day it happened. As Lana quickly discovers, however, her abduction is not even the most alarming part of her situation. To her shock, she soon learns that she is to be stripped naked and sold as a slave to the highest bidder.

When she resists the intimate, deeply humiliating procedures necessary to prepare her for the auction, Lana merely earns herself a long, hard, bare-bottom spanking, but her passionate defiance catches the attention of her captor and results in a change in his plans. Instead of being sold, Lana will be given as a gift to Dante, the region's powerful king.

Dante makes it abundantly clear that he will expect absolute obedience and that any misbehavior will be dealt with sternly, yet in spite of everything Lana cannot help feeling safe and cared for in the handsome ruler's arms. Even when Dante's punishments leave her with flaming cheeks and a bottom sore from more than just a spanking, it only sets her desire for him burning hotter.

But though Dante's dominant lovemaking brings her pleasure beyond anything she ever imagined, Lana fears she may never be more than a plaything to him, and her fears soon lead to rebellion. When an escape attempt goes awry and she is captured by Dante's most dangerous enemy, she is left to wonder if her master cares for her enough to come to her rescue. Will the king risk everything to reclaim what is his, and if he does bring his human girl home safe and sound, can he find a way to teach Lana once and for all that she belongs to him completely?

A Gift for the Doctor

After allowing herself to be taken captive in order to save her friends, Morgana awakens to find herself naked, bound, and at the mercy of a handsome doctor named Kade. She cannot hide her helpless arousal as her captor takes his time thoroughly examining her bare body, but when she disobeys him she quickly discovers that defiance will earn her a sound spanking.

His stern chastisement and bold dominance awaken desires within her that she never knew existed, but Morgana is shocked when she learns the truth about Kade. As a powerful shifter and the alpha of his pack, he has been ordered by the evil lord who took Morgana prisoner to claim her and sire children with her in order to combine the strength of their two bloodlines.

Kade's true loyalties lie with the rebels seeking to overthrow the tyrant, however, and he has his own reasons for desiring Morgana as his mate. Though submitting to a dominant alpha does not come easily to a woman who was once her kingdom's most powerful sorceress, Kade's masterful lovemaking is unlike anything she has experienced before, and soon enough she is aching for his touch. But with civil war on the verge of engulfing the capital, will Morgana be torn from the arms of the man she loves or will she stand and fight at his side no matter the cost?

A Gift for the Commander

After she is rescued from a cruel tyrant and brought to the planet Terranovum, Olivia soon discovers that she is to be auctioned to the highest bidder. But before she can be sold, she must be trained, and the man who will train her is none other than the commander of the king's army.

Wes has tamed many human females, and when Olivia resists his efforts to bathe her in preparation for her initial inspection, he strips the beautiful, feisty girl bare and spanks her soundly. His stern chastisement leaves Olivia tearful and repentant yet undeniably aroused, and after the punishment she cannot resist begging for her new master's touch.

Once she has been examined Olivia's training begins in earnest, and Wes takes her to his bed to teach her what it means to belong to a dominant man. But try as he might, he cannot bring himself to see Olivia as just another slave. She touches his heart in a way he thought nothing could, and with each passing day he grows more certain that he must claim her as his own. But with war breaking out across Terranovum, can Wes protect both his world and his woman?

Kept for Christmas

After Raina LeBlanc shows up for a meeting unprepared because she was watching naughty videos late at night instead of working, she finds herself in trouble with Dr. Eliot Knight, her stern, handsome boss. He makes it clear that she is in need of strict discipline, and soon she is lying over his knee for a painful, embarrassing bare-bottom spanking.

Though her helpless display of arousal during the punishment fills Raina with shame, she is both excited and comforted when Eliot takes her in his arms after it is over, and when he invites her to spend the upcoming Christmas holiday with him she happily agrees. But is she prepared to offer him the complete submission he demands?

Wedded to the Warriors

As an unauthorized third child, nineteen-year-old Aimee Harrington has spent her life avoiding discovery by government authorities, but her world comes crashing down around her after she is caught stealing a vehicle in an act of petulant rebellion. Within hours of her arrest, she is escorted onto a ship bound for a detention center in the far reaches of the solar system.

This facility is no ordinary prison, however. It is a training center for future brides, and once Aimee has been properly prepared, she will be intimately, shamefully examined and then sold to an alien male in need of a mate. Worse still, Aimee's defiant attitude quickly earns her the wrath of the strict warden, and to make an example of her, Aimee is offered as a wife not to a sophisticated gentleman but to three huge, fiercely dominant warriors of the planet Ollorin.

Though Ollorin males are considered savages on Earth, Aimee soon realizes that while her new mates will demand her obedience and will not hesitate to spank her soundly if her behavior warrants it, they will also cherish and protect her in a way she has never experienced before. But when the time comes for her men to master her completely, will she find herself begging for more as her beautiful body is claimed hard and thoroughly by all three of them at once?

The Warrior's Little Princess

Irena cannot remember who she is, where she came from, or how she ended up alone in a dark forest wearing only a nightgown, but none of that matters as much as the fact that the vile creatures holding her captive seem intent on having her for dinner. Fate intervenes, however, when a mysterious, handsome warrior arrives in the nick of time to save her.

Darrius has always known that one day he would be forced by the power within him to claim a woman, and after he rescues the beautiful, innocent Irena he decides to make her his own. But the feisty girl will require more than just the protection Darrius can offer. She will need both his gentle, loving care and his firm hand applied to her bare bottom whenever she is naughty.

Irena soon finds herself quivering with desire as Darrius masters her virgin body completely, and she delights in her new life as his little girl. But Darrius is much more than an ordinary sellsword, and being his wife will mean belonging to him utterly, to be taken hard and often in even the most shameful of ways. When the truth of her own identity is revealed at last, will she still choose to remain by his side?

Her Alien Doctors

After nineteen-year-old Jenny Monroe is caught stealing from the home of a powerful politician, she is sent to a special prison in deep space to be trained for her future role as an alien's bride.

Despite the public bare-bottom spanking she receives upon her arrival at the detention center, Jenny remains defiant, and before long she earns herself a trip to the notorious medical wing of the facility. Once there, Jenny quickly discovers that a sore bottom will now be the least of her worries, and soon enough she is naked, restrained, and shamefully on display as three stern, handsome alien doctors examine and correct her in the most humiliating ways imaginable.

The doctors are experts in the treatment of naughty young women, and as Jenny is brought ever closer to the edge of a shattering climax only to be denied again and again, she finds herself begging to be taken in any way they please. But will her captors be content to give Jenny up once her punishment is over, or will they decide to make her their own and master her completely?

Taming Their Pet

When the scheming of her father's political enemies makes it impossible to continue hiding the fact that she is an unauthorized third child, twenty-year-old Isabella Bedard is sent to a detainment facility in deep space where she will be prepared for her new life as an alien's bride.

Her situation is made far worse after some ill-advised mischief forces the strict warden to ensure that she is sold as quickly as possible, and before she knows it, Isabella is standing naked before two huge, roughly handsome alien men, helpless and utterly on display for their inspection. More disturbing still, the men make it clear that they are buying her not as a bride, but as a pet.

Zack and Noah have made a career of taming even the most headstrong of females, and they waste no time in teaching their new pet that her absolute obedience will be expected and even the slightest defiance will earn her a painful, embarrassing bare-bottom spanking, along with far more humiliating punishments if her behavior makes it necessary.

Over the coming weeks, Isabella is trained as a pony and as a kitten, and she learns what it means to fully surrender her body to the bold dominance of two men who will not hesitate to claim her in any way they please. But though she cannot deny her helpless arousal at being so thoroughly mastered, can she truly allow herself to fall in love with men who keep her as a pet?

Sold to the Beasts

As an unauthorized third child with parents who were more interested in their various criminal enterprises than they were in her, Michelle Carter is used to feeling unloved, but it still hurts when she is brought to another world as a bride for two men who turn out not to even want one.

After Roan and Dane lost the woman they loved, they swore there would never be anyone else, and when their closest friend purchases a beautiful human he hopes will become their wife, they reject the match. Though they are cursed to live as outcasts who shift into terrible beasts, they are not heartless, so they offer Michelle a place in their home alongside the other servants. She will have food, shelter, and all she needs, but discipline will be strict and their word will be law.

Michelle soon puts Roan and Dane to the test, and when she disobeys them her bottom is bared for a deeply humiliating public spanking. Despite her situation, the punishment leaves her shamefully aroused and longing for her new masters to make her theirs, and as the days pass they find that she has claimed a place in their hearts as well. But when the same enemy who took their first love threatens to tear Roan and Dane away from her, will Michele risk her life to intervene?

Mated to the Dragons

After she uncovers evidence of a treasonous conspiracy by the most powerful man on Earth, Jada Rivers ends up framed for a terrible crime, shipped off to a detention facility in deep space, and kept in solitary confinement until she can be sold as a bride. But the men who purchase her are no ordinary aliens. They are dragons, the kings of Draegira, and she will be their shared mate.

Bruddis and Draego are captivated by Jada, but before she can become their queen the beautiful, feisty little human will need to be publicly claimed, thoroughly trained, and put to the test in the most shameful manner imaginable. If she will not yield her body and her heart to them completely, the fire in their blood will burn out of control until it destroys the brotherly bond between them, putting their entire world at risk of a cataclysmic war.

Though Jada is shocked by the demands of her dragon kings, she is left helplessly aroused by their stern dominance. With her virgin body quivering with need, she cannot bring herself to resist as they take her hard and savagely in any way they please. But can she endure the trials before her and claim her place at their side, or will her stubborn defiance bring Draegira to ruin?

Conquered

I've lived in hiding since the Vakarrans arrived, helping my band of human survivors evade the aliens who now rule our world with an iron fist. But my luck ran out.

Captured by four of their fiercest warriors, I know what comes next. They'll make an example of me, to show how even the most defiant human can be broken, trained, and mastered.

I promise myself that I'll prove them wrong, that I'll never yield, even when I'm stripped bare, publicly shamed, and used in the most humiliating way possible.

But my body betrays me.

My will to resist falters as these brutes share me between the four of them and I can't help but wonder if soon, they will conquer my heart…

Mastered

First the Vakarrans took my home. Then they took my sister. Now, they have taken me.

As a prisoner of four of their fiercest warriors, I know what fate awaits me. Humans who dare to fight back the way I did are not just punished, they are taught their place in ways so shameful I shudder to think about them.

The four huge, intimidating alien brutes who took me captive are going to claim me in every way possible, using me more thoroughly than I can imagine. I despise them, yet as they force one savage, shattering climax after another from my naked, quivering body, I cannot help but wonder if soon I will beg for them to master me completely.

Abducted

When I left Earth behind to become a Celestial Mate, I was promised a perfect match. But four Vakarrans decided they wanted me, and Vakarrans don't ask for what they want, they take it.

These fearsome, savagely sexy alien warriors don't care what some computer program thinks would be best for me. They've claimed me as their mate, and soon they will claim my body.

I planned to resist, but after I was stripped bare and shamefully punished, they teased me until at last I pleaded for the climax I'd been so cruelly denied. When I broke, I broke completely. Now they are going to do absolutely anything they please with me, and I'm going to beg for all of it.

Ravaged

Though the aliens were the ones I always feared, it was my own kind who hurt me. Men took me captive, and it was four Vakarran warriors who saved me. But they don't plan to set me free…

I belong to them now, and they intend to make me theirs more thoroughly than I can imagine.

They are the enemy, and first I try to fight, then I try to run. But as they punish me, claim me, and share me between them, it isn't long before I am begging them to ravage me completely.

Feral

He told me to stay away from him, that if I got too close he would not be able to stop himself. He would pin me down and take me so fiercely my throat would be sore from screaming before he finished wringing one savage, desperate climax after another from my helpless, quivering body.

Part of me was terrified, but another part needed to know if he would truly throw me to the ground, mount me, and rut me like a wild animal, longer and harder than any human ever could.

Now, as the feral beast flips me over to claim me even more shamefully when I've already been used more thoroughly than I imagined possible, I wonder if I should have listened to him…

Subdued

The resistance sent them, but that's not really why these four battle-hardened Vakarrans are here.

They came for me. To conquer me. To master me. To ravage me. To strip me bare, punish me for the slightest hint of defiance, and use my quivering virgin body in ways far beyond anything in even the very darkest of my dreams, until I've been utterly, completely, and shamefully subdued.

I vow never to beg for mercy, but I can't help wondering how long it will be until I beg for more.

Consumed

I thought I knew how to handle a man like him, but there are no men like him. Though he is a billionaire, when he desired me he did not try to buy me, and when he wanted me bared and bound he didn't call his bodyguards. He did it himself, even as I fought him, because he could.

He told me soon I would beg him to ravage me… and I did. But it wasn't the pain of his belt searing my naked backside that drove me to plead with him to use me so shamefully I might never stop blushing. I begged because my body knew its master, and it didn't give me a choice.

But my body is not all he plans to claim. He wants my mind and my soul too, and he will have them. He's going to take so much of me there will be nothing left. He's going to consume me.

Frenzy

Inside the walls I was a respected scientist. Out here I'm vulnerable, desperate, and soon to be at the mercy of the beasts and barbarians who rule these harsh lands. But that is not the worst of it.

When the suppressants that keep my shameful secret wear off, overwhelming, unimaginable need will take hold of me completely. I'm about to go into heat, and I know what comes next…

But I'm not the only one with instincts far beyond my control. Savage men roam this wilderness, driven by their very nature to claim a female like me more fiercely than I can imagine, paying no heed to my screams as one brutal climax after another is ripped from my helplessly willing body.

It won't be long now, and when the mating starts, it will be nothing short of a frenzy.

Frantic

Naked, bound, and helplessly on display, my arousal drips down my bare thighs and pools at my feet as the entire city watches, waiting for the inevitable. I'm going into heat, and they know it.

When the feral beasts who live outside the walls find me, they will show my virgin body no mercy. With my need growing more desperate by the second, I'm not sure I'll want them to…

By the time the brutes arrive to claim and ravage me, I'm going to be absolutely frantic.

Fever

I've led the Omegaborn for years, but the moment these brutes arrived from beyond the wall I knew everything was about to change. These beasts aren't here to take orders from me, they're here to take me the way I was meant to be taken, no matter how desperately I resist what I need.

Naked, punished, and sore, all I can do is scream out one savage, shameful climax after another as my body is claimed, used, and mastered. I'm about to learn what it means to be an omega…

Manhandled

Two hours ago, my ship reached the docks at Dryac.

An hour ago, a slaver tried to drag me into an alley.

Fifty-nine minutes ago, a beast of a man knocked him out cold.

Fifty-eight minutes ago, I told my rescuer to screw off, I could take care of myself.

Fifty-five minutes ago, I felt a thick leather belt on my bare backside for the first time.

Forty-five minutes ago, I started begging.

Thirty minutes ago, he bent me over a crate and claimed me in the most shameful way possible.

Twenty-nine minutes ago, I started screaming.

Twenty-five minutes ago, I climaxed with a crowd watching and my bottom sore inside and out.

Twenty-four minutes ago, I realized he was nowhere near done with me.

One minute ago, he finally decided I'd learned my lesson, for the moment at least.

As he leads me away, naked, well-punished, and very thoroughly used, he tells me I work for him now, I'll have to earn the privilege of clothing, and I'm his to enjoy as often as he pleases.

Fear

She wasn't supposed to be there tonight. I took her because I had no other choice, but as I carried her from her home dripping wet and wearing nothing but a towel, I knew I would be keeping her.

I'm going to make her tell me everything I need to know. Then I'm going to make her mine.

She'll sob as my belt lashes her bottom and she'll scream as climax after savage climax is forced from her naked, quivering body, but there will be no mercy no matter how shamefully she begs.

She's not just going to learn to obey me. She's going to learn to fear me.

Marked

I know how to handle men who won't take no for an answer, but Silas isn't a man. He's a beast who takes what he wants, as long and hard and savagely as he pleases, and tonight he wants me.

He's not even pretending he's going to be gentle. He's going to ravage me, and it's going to hurt.

I'll be spanked into quivering submission and used thoroughly and shamefully, but even when the endless series of helpless, screaming climaxes is finally over, I won't just be sore and spent.

I will be marked.

My body will no longer be mine. It will be his to use, his to enjoy, and his to breed, and no matter how desperate my need might grow in his absence, it will respond to his touch alone.

Forever.

Prize

Exiled from Earth by a tyrannical government, I was meant to be sold for use on a distant world. But Vane doesn't buy things. When he wants something, he takes it, and I was no different.

This alien brute didn't just strip me, punish me, and claim me with his whole crew watching. He broke me, making me beg for mercy and then for far more shameful things. Perhaps he would've been gentle if I hadn't defied him in front of his men, but I doubt it. He's not the gentle type.

When he carried me aboard his ship naked, blushing, and sore, I thought I would be no more than a trophy to be shown off or a plaything to amuse him until he tired of me, but I was wrong.

He took me as a prize, but he's keeping me as his mate.

On Her Knees

Blaire Conrad isn't just the most popular girl at Stonewall Academy. She's a queen who reigns over her subjects with an iron fist. But she's made me an enemy, and I don't play by her rules.

I make the rules, and I punish my enemies.

She'll scream and beg as I strip her, spank her, and force one brutal climax after another from her beautiful little body, but before I'm done with her she'll beg me shamefully for so much more.

It's time for the king to teach his queen her place.

Boss

The moment Brooke Mikaels walked into my office, I knew she was mine. She needed my help and thought she could use her sweet little body to get it, but she learned a hard lesson instead.

I don't make deals with silly little girls. I spank them.

She'll get what she needs, but first she'll moan and beg and scream with each brutal climax as she takes everything I give her. She belongs to me now, and soon she'll know what that means.

His Majesty

Maximo Giovanni Santaro is a king. A real king, like in the old days. The kind I didn't know still existed. The kind who commands obedience and punishes any hint of defiance from his subjects.

His Majesty doesn't take no for an answer, and refusing his royal command has earned me not just a spanking that will leave me sobbing, but a lesson so utterly shameful that it will serve as an example for anyone else who might dare to disobey him. I will beg and plead as one brutal, screaming climax after another ravages my quivering body, but there will be no mercy for me.

He's not going to stop until he's taught me that my rightful place is at his feet, naked and wet.